SIX-GUN KILL

"Last chance," Morgan said quietly. "Tell me what I want to know." Morgan drew his knife and Canty tried to look away from it. "I don't have much time, so listen good. I can castrate you, cut your eyes out, or make you deaf and dumb with this. I can fix your legs so you'll never walk again."

Canty's eyes crossed as Morgan touched the bridge of his nose with the point of the knife. Morgan's voice became quieter than it had been. "You'll feel pain like you never imagined, pain so bad you'll beg me to kill you, and you won't die of the pain. You don't want to go through that, so tell me before I start."

Morgan's voice dropped to a whisper. "After what you did to that woman, I don't know that I'll want to stop."

Also in the *Buckskin* Series:
BUCKSKIN #1: RIFLE RIVER
BUCKSKIN #2: GUNSTOCK
BUCKSKIN #3: PISTOLTOWN
BUCKSKIN #4: COLT CREEK
BUCKSKIN #5: GUNSIGHT GAP
BUCKSKIN #6: TRIGGER SPRING
BUCKSKIN #7: CARTRIDGE COAST
BUCKSKIN #8: HANGFIRE HILL
BUCKSKIN #9: CROSSFIRE COUNTRY
BUCKSKIN #10: BOLT-ACTION
BUCKSKIN #11: TRIGGER GUARD
BUCKSKIN #12: RECOIL
BUCKSKIN #13: GUNPOINT
BUCKSKIN #14: LEVER ACTION
BUCKSKIN #15: SCATTERGUN
BUCKSKIN #16: WINCHESTER VALLEY
BUCKSKIN #17: GUNSMOKE GORGE
BUCKSKIN #18: REMINGTON RIDGE
BUCKSKIN #19: SHOTGUN STATION
BUCKSKIN #20: PISTOL GRIP
BUCKSKIN #21: PEACEMAKER PASS
BUCKSKIN #22: SILVER CITY CARBINE
BUCKSKIN #23: CALIFORNIA CROSSFIRE
BUCKSKIN #24: COLT CROSSING
BUCKSKIN #25: POWDER CHARGE
BUCKSKIN #26: LARAMIE SHOWDOWN
BUCKSKIN #27: DOUBLE ACTION
BUCKSKIN #28: APACHE RIFLES
BUCKSKIN #29: RETURN FIRE
BUCKSKIN #30: RIMFIRE REVENGE
BUCKSKIN #31: TOMBSTONE TEN GAUGE
BUCKSKIN #32: DEATH DRAW
BUCKSKIN #33: .52 CALIBER SHOOT-OUT
BUCKSKIN #34: TRICK SHOOTER
BUCKSKIN #35: PISTOL WHIPPED
BUCKSKIN #36: HOGLEG HELL
BUCKSKIN #37: COLT .45 VENGEANCE
BUCKSKIN #38: DERRINGER DANGER
BUCKSKIN #39: BLAZING SIX-GUNS

BUCKSKIN #40

SIX-GUN KILL

KIT DALTON

LEISURE BOOKS  NEW YORK CITY

A LEISURE BOOK®

July 2006

Published by

Dorchester Publishing Co., Inc.
200 Madison Avenue
New York, NY 10016

ISBN 0-8439-3637-1

Printed in the United States of America.

Visit us on the web at www.dorchesterpub.com.

SIX-GUN KILL

Chapter One

No more than five minutes for a change of horses, the company rule book said, and they were sticking pretty close to that in most of the change stations along the line. Only in one place called Yamahaw did they go over ten, and that was because the station keeper was so drunk he could barely stand and had trouble getting fresh horses out of the corral.

Even so, they were rolling again in twelve minutes. Not so bad, Morgan thought, settling back in the jolting coach, though he could see how delays like that could add up over several hundred miles of road. But that wasn't his business. If the contract with Butterfield went through, he'd be supplying horses for this stretch of road, not calling down station keepers for being drunk and slow.

He'd been riding the stage since it pulled out of McHargville at four o'clock that morning. Now it was getting on noon, and he was tired and dirty. There was no way to stay clean while riding a stage in hot, dusty country, but being so tired was his own doing. A quick cup of coffee and a splash of water on his face was all Morgan could manage after he ran from the whore's bed to catch the stage. The driver was yelling his last call when he got there. He could have stayed over and taken the next stage, but business was business and it was time to get moving.

Morgan opened his eyes and looked out at the Nevada desert. It sure as hell didn't look like Idaho, not a tree in sight. Seemed like the only things that grew here were sagebrush and greasewood. Far off there were snowcapped mountains. Alkali dust blew in the hot wind, covering the stage and its passengers with a gray film as fine as flour. Morgan felt it in the back of his throat and thought of cold beer. Lord but he was tired and thirsty.

The other passengers, two middle-aged men in business suits, rode like experienced travelers, absorbing the jolting of the stage without trying to get too comfortable. Morgan couldn't tell if they were asleep. Their eyes were closed. At least they didn't talk. Both were going all the way to Carson City, Morgan's own destination, and it would be hell to have to listen to their stories over so many miles. One of them looked like a high-class drummer. The other man he couldn't place. Just as long as they didn't talk about the fascinating lives they led.

Normally, Morgan didn't mind trading bullshit. It helped to while away the time. Today was different: he was tired. That whore, Marie, back in McHargville, was enough to give a man a sore cock, and that was what he had, not that he was complaining. It had been worth every stroke of his shaft. No way in the world a man could complain about what Marie had done: the soreness was due to him keeping at it so long. If truth be told, she had even cautioned him to take it easy, but of course he didn't. Back in Idaho, working like the devil on his horse ranch, he had gone a full nine weeks without a woman, and that was enough to make a man want to screw a mountain goat. After mounting Marie for the umpteenth time, she had asked if there were any more like him at home, and when he said she ought to see his Uncle Jethro, they laughed about it and went on from there.

Hence, the sore cock.

Damn! He was hungry as well as tired. McHargville, where he'd allowed himself no time to eat, was about 250 miles from Carson City, which meant the trip would take two full days. Average traveling time for a coach on a good road was between 100 and 125 miles a day. So said the booklet that William Butterfield had sent him in the mail along with his first letter. The booklet was yellow with age and told of the glories of the original Butterfield Stage Line founded by his father, the famous John Butterfield, now rich and retired. Old John had kept the Nevada line so his illegitimate son, William, could manage it. This information came from the manager of the Idaho bank, where Morgan had an outstanding loan. The manager was glad to hear that Morgan was doing something about paying it off.

It looked like the horse deal with Butterfield would make it possible to do that. Butterfield had placed a notice inviting bids from relay horse suppliers in a number of newspapers. Morgan made what he thought was a good bid and enclosed a letter of reference from the skinflint at the bank. This led to other letters, and now he was heading for Carson City with Butterfield's final letter of acceptance in his pocket. Unless something went wrong, and why should it, he'd be able to get the bank off his back and put his Spade Bit horse ranch back in the black.

Now, eating dust as the coach jolted and swayed on its way to Carson City, Morgan decided that he had no great love for the stage line business. Cheer up, he told himself, you're just tired and hungry and have a sore cock. He chuckled when he thought of how hard he'd worked to earn his sore dingus, his badge of honor. Across from him, the man he couldn't place opened his eyes and gave him a look. Morgan turned the chuckle into a cough and closed his eyes. Conversation—any kind of chin music—was the last thing he wanted. Once, while on a train, he had said nice day to a fellow passenger and suffered a harangue about the changeable nature of the weather for the next thirty miles. But how could you tell a nun to button up her fucking lip?

Come to think of it, he'd been in much the same condition then as now. Worn out from too much cunt. But at least he hadn't been hungry. There would be a lunch stop coming soon, but he didn't look forward to it. Stage food was not as bad as the chain gang, not as good as the army. You'd think a man on the verge of an important business venture wouldn't get himself into these fixes. Well, he had worked night and day for nine weeks, had gone without a woman all that time, so there was some excuse for it. And if there were no hitches, if the contract got signed and money changed hands, then he'd be working even harder.

The contract was to be for one year. It could be renewed for another year, or longer, if the business arrangement proved to be to their mutual satisfaction. That was how Butterfield talked in his letters. Morgan didn't mind that. Let him talk any way he liked as long as he kept up his end of the deal.

Butterfield had mentioned trouble with stage robbers in his final letter. That was the one in which he had suggested that Morgan ride the stage over the miles of road he'd be providing horses for. "To obtain some firsthand knowledge of how the business works." Morgan knew pretty well how the business worked, but he did it anyway, boarding the stage at McHargville, the end of his stretch of road. Nothing he had seen so far added to his knowledge of the stage line business. He was more interested in stage robbers.

According to Butterfield, the trouble with these robbers had been "sporadic." Butterfield didn't say how bad the trouble was, or if he thought it was the work of more than one gang. What he was doing, "in all honesty," he had said, was letting Morgan know that he had to be prepared for some trouble. Morgan didn't like men who told him things "in all honesty," but that didn't have to mean a man who talked like that was a crook. Whatever it meant, he would have to get used to it, and if he couldn't do that he could always pull out and go home. Provided he got paid, of course. He was not about to go back to Idaho with empty pockets. Butterfield might be a slick operator, but he'd pay up or get his ear pasted to his head with the barrel of a six-gun.

Whoa there, Morgan told himself. He hadn't even met the man yet and here he was giving him a fat ear. Just the same, there was a lot riding on this, no getting away from that. Spade Bit had never fully recovered from the Jack Mormon raid a couple of years back. The renegade fanatics had burned his house and outbuildings, slaughtered the stock they didn't take, and killed the few men left to guard the place. He had to go far to pay it back, but there was no money at the end of it, and he had to start all over again. Hard work, a bank loan, and men who worked on trust put him back in business. Even so, money was always a problem. There always came a time when he had to leave the ranch to see what he could scratch together in the outside world. Men had to be paid; other expenses had to be met. If you couldn't do that, you might as well quit, find a job, and work for wages.

So far he'd managed to hang on, building up his stock as best he could. No little credit belonged to his top hand, Sid Sefton, a man among men. Sid looked after the ranch when Morgan was away. And it could not have been in better hands. Right now there was no place Morgan would rather have been than back at Spade Bit, but that would have to wait. As soon as the contract was signed, he would drive his horses down from Idaho. He would need the advance payment, agreed upon in Butterfield's letter, to buy additional horses from other ranchers.

"Lunchtime!" the driver was yelling from up on the box. "Luncheon is bein' served!" All stage drivers thought they were cards. And most of them were called Ben or Curly; the names seemed to go with the job. This driver, Curly, was telling them to hurry it up. He was well into his sixties, but Morgan couldn't fault the way he handled the horses. The shotgun guard, a man of fifty or so, didn't laugh at the driver's jokes, and neither did anyone else. Morgan climbed down, but he didn't hurry. The kind of food waiting inside the station didn't call for hurry. What wasn't eaten up today would be served up tomorrow, and so on down to the end of the week.

The station buildings were long, low adobes with grass and weeds growing out of sod roofs. This was a main station, and it had a barn and a stable for about fifteen horses, a bunk room for the station keeper and his hostlers, and an eating room for passengers. The two men from the coach got down after Morgan, but the drummer stayed outside, sat on a rock, and ate sandwiches from a paper sack. Near the door was a tin basin of water, a flour sack and a cake of yellow soap. Morgan didn't stop to wash his hands, and neither did the other man.

Inside, the floor was hard-packed dirt. The table was a wide board laid across two barrels. Lunch was boiled bacon and beans dished onto battered tin plates. A pint of coffee in a tin mug, no milk, no sugar, came with the lunch. There was mustard for the bacon and a bowl of salt for those who thought the meat wasn't salty enough. The station keeper, a youngish man with a bald head and a droopy mustache, sawed off slices from a stale brown loaf. It sounded like he was sawing wood. He served the driver and the guard when they came in and said something about horses. He had some kind of foreign accent. Outside, the stablemen were changing the horses. The driver forked in bacon and beans, smacking his lips, allowing as how this was better truck than they got at "Fuckingham Palace." There were no ladies present so he could make a joke like that. Across from Morgan the man from the coach ate like he was doing penance. Morgan drank the coffee, but passed on the bacon after he got a whiff of it. Better to go hungry another day than to retaste that bacon every time the coach hit a rock in the road.

They got going again. No use trying to sleep with a growling belly, a jolting coach. There wouldn't be a change of horses for another twenty-five miles. On this stretch of road, which was considered "good," they changed the horses every twenty-five miles. On the bad roads they changed every eight miles. After the contract was signed, on his way back to Idaho, he would stop off at McHargville and talk to the superintendent of this division, Frank C. Eaton. Though Morgan had seen his name above the door of the stage office, he hadn't gone in to see Eaton because he had no authority until the contract was signed. He didn't know how Eaton would take him. The division superintendent ran his 250 miles of road like a petty tyrant. He purchased the horses, mules, harnesses, and food for men and beasts. He built station buildings and dug wells. He paid the station keepers, hostlers, divers, guards, blacksmiths, and fired them when he chose. There might be trouble with Frank C. Eaton, but Morgan thought he could handle it.

Frank C. Eaton could wait. Morgan found himself thinking of Marie, the whore who had said she was "Frinch." "I'm Frinch an' I know all the Finch ways a pleasurin' a man." "I just love your thang, cowboy," was something else she'd said. Well, sir, he just loved her thang as much as she loved his. . . .

A young woman—maybe not so young, maybe about twenty-eight—boarded the stage at the next change station. Back of the station a collection of houses and shacks straggled along the side of a hill. A mining camp that wasn't doing too well, Morgan figured. It had none of the machinery that the big companies had put in where there was money to be made. The woman had blue eyes, dark brown hair, a pleasant face. She carried a large canvas grip and a tin lunch box like the ones miners ate from. Somebody, no doubt the woman, had painted the lunch box blue and decorated it with painted yellow flowers, but it remained unmistakably a lunch box. Morgan liked the look of that lunch box.

The drummer and the other man opened their eyes long enough to look at the woman, then went back to their dozing. She was no beauty so they weren't interested. Morgan thought the young woman and her lunchbox looked fine, and he helped her get settled beside him on the seat. The fresh smell of soap she gave off made him feel like an unwashed saloon swamper, but he guessed the coach itself smelled worse than he did. It had the usual stink of hair grease, sweat, stale underwear, and tobacco.

"My name is Margaret Deakin," she said. Her slimness made her look taller than she was. She wore a simple gray dress and laced boots with dust on them. Soon she'd be as dusty as the rest of them, so the gray dress was a good choice for stage travel.

"Morgan," she said when he told her his name. "That sounds Welsh. I'm of Welsh descent myself, and my intended's name is Llewellyn Owens. I'm on my way to be married."

That was one way of keeping him at arm's length. In his time he'd met women who told him they were either married or engaged. A few went so far as to hint how jealous and dangerous their men were. He'd fucked more than a few of those women, but he was pretty sure this Margaret Deakin wasn't like that. She was just making conversation.

"The best of luck to both of you," he said.

They had grown up together in the same small town in Ohio. Now Owens was an assayer in a mining camp about a hundred miles down the road. She had been keeping house for her father, who was working a claim at the town where she got on the stage. They had been in Nevada for more than a year.

"Yelverton's pretty well played out," she said, "but my father insists on staying there. He can manage perfectly well without me. He's only sixty-six, in good health, and he has a railroad pension as well as the income from a hardware store my brother still runs. It's not as if I'm deserting him. He's been talking about marrying a half-Indian woman whose husband got run over by an ore wagon."

Morgan hoped the half-Indian wouldn't take the old boy to the creek and wash the money out of him. As if reading his mind, Margaret Deakin said, "She's a nice, sensible woman; I think they'll be all right. Are you married, Mr. Morgan?"

"Never got around to it," Morgan said, giving his standard answer to a bothersome question. Women thought all men should be married. Some could get pretty acid about men they thought were shirking their "responsibilities." "I've often thought about it, still do. One of these days. . . ."

She laughed at him. "You're fibbing, Mr. Morgan." They both laughed. "You were going to say one of these days I'm going to meet the right girl, et cetera. Admit it: you haven't the slightest intention of getting married."

"I admit it," Morgan said.

"What you don't know is, the right girl is going to find you, not the other way around. Then you're going to find yourself the prisoner of love, believe me."

Morgan didn't believe her: the last time he'd been a prisoner of love Andrew Johnson was president. "You could be right," he said.

"I know I'm right," she said confidently.

Her conversation was scattershot. "The miners call Llewellyn Lew and he hates it," she was saying now.

Morgan thought Llewellyn ought to be glad that's all they called him. For some reason he got a picture of

Llewellyn as a prissy stiffneck. Maybe this feisty young woman could take some of the starch out of him.

"We're Campbellites," she said. "Very strict, at least Llewellyn is. You know what a Campbellite is?"

"Sort of like an offshoot Baptist."

"Close enough. My father was very strict until my mother died, then he said the hell with it and hasn't been to church since. Not only that, he drinks six bottles of beer every Saturday night and thinks he wants to marry a half-Indian woman."

"He's bound straight for hell," Morgan said.

"How do you like my watch?" she said, meaning the lapel watch pinned to her dress. "I'll show it to you." She unpinned the watch and pressed the button that opened the face cover. Inscribed on the inside of the lid was: *To Margaret, with deep affection, Llewellyn.*

"It's very nice," Morgan said. Why couldn't the stiffneck just say he loved the woman?

"Would you like a sandwich?" she said next, opening the top of the lunch box. "I have six sandwiches in here—three chicken, three ham—and there is no way I'm going to eat all of them. Oh, I'll eat something later, but I'm too excited to eat right now. Eat something, please—they'll go bad in the heat if somebody doesn't eat them."

"I might try one," Morgan said.

"Chicken or ham? Nevada chicken tends to be tough, but it's all right if you boil it first, then give it a short time in the oven to give it a roasted taste. I'd never have packed so much food except my father is a big eater and thinks everybody else ought to be."

God bless Mr. Deakin, Morgan thought. "Chicken would be fine," he said.

The first sandwich she gave him was wrapped in oiled paper like the others. The meat was tender, and the bread was fresh. "I baked it myself," Margaret Deakin said. There was enough chicken to make three sandwiches, and it tasted ten times better than anything you could get in a restaurant.

Morgan forced himself to eat another sandwich. He forced himself like a starving wolf in a sheepfold. This one was ham, and it was as thick and juicy as the first. Once again he blessed Mr. Deakin and his daughter and even included the half-Indian woman, in case she'd had a hand in making these sandwiches.

"Thanks and thanks again," he said when she tried him with yet another sandwich, "but I couldn't eat another bite. I'll never eat better sandwiches if I live to be a hundred. Have to admit it: I was starving. Anyway, darned hungry."

"I could tell," she said. "I told you you should be married. Then your wife could pack sandwiches for you."

After a while she fell asleep, her head bobbing over on his shoulder, and he figured she might have been up half the night, getting ready for this journey. He didn't think he was sentimental or softhearted, far from it, but it wasn't just the sandwiches that made him like her so much. Most of the women he'd known were whores or civil ladies panting for cock, and it was a nice change to meet a woman who was neither. With the rough life he led, always having to watch his back, there were times when he had to remind himself that the world wasn't completely filled with greedy, self-seeking sons of bitches. That was obvious to anyone but a black-hearted bastard, yet it was easy enough to lose sight of it.

Well fed, his sour mood gone, Morgan finally dozed off.

Chapter Two

It was getting dark when the stage pulled into the change station. Margaret Deakin woke up rubbing her eyes, saying to Morgan, "I hope I have enough time to answer a call of nature."

"Take all the time you want," Morgan said, thinking he'd kick the driver's bony ass if he made any outhouse jokes. He was helping her down, and the driver was yelling at the station keeper to show his face, when five men wearing miners' clothes, their faces masked by bandannas, came out of the station building with guns in their hands. Two of them moved forward to get in front of the horses to keep them from bolting. Two of them shot the guard and the driver off the box. They shot the guard first because he had a shotgun. The last man raised a sawed-off shotgun and held it on Morgan and Margaret Deakin.

"Drop your gun, or I'll kill the woman," he shouted.

Morgan had his gun out, but Margaret Deakin was in front of him, and there was nothing he could do. The man with the sawed-off moved them back with gestures, picked up Morgan's gun, then shouted for the drummer and the other man to step down. As soon as they did, he pulled a pistol from his belt and killed them with two shots. It was all quick and easy, as if they'd done it before and had practiced doing it. Morgan wondered why they hadn't killed him. They had his gun; there was nothing stopping them.

It was hard to see what they looked like because of poor lighting. The man with the sawed-off was very big, sort of clumsy in his movements, though there was nothing clumsy about the way he killed the drummer and the other man. Morgan thought he sounded like a Scotchman. The few Scotchmen he knew all sounded alike. He didn't know why he was trying to fix that in his mind. If the big man with the Scotch accent didn't kill him, the others would do it in a minute. No reason they wouldn't kill him after they'd killed four other men. But when he looked at them in the thickening light, he saw they had their guns back in their holsters and some of them were laughing. They moved forward, still laughing, more interested in the woman than they were in him. He knew then what was going to happen to her, and there was nothing he could do about it except get himself killed.

They moved closer. It seemed like they were taking their time, but that was wrong. They were moving right quick, some of them still laughing. One of them had little oval-shaped eyeglasses with wire frames. He was grinning instead of laughing as he looked at Margaret Deakin. His ears stuck out. Morgan wanted to remember the jug ears and the little oval-shaped eyeglasses. He didn't know what good it would do him, trying to fix on things like that, but he wasn't dead yet; they hadn't killed him yet.

Now there were four of them crowding in close, all but the man who was keeping the horses in place. Odd thing was there was nothing of the desperado about them, not even about the big man with the sawed-off who shouted so loud. Except for the Scotch accent and the jug ears, there was nothing distinctive about the men. Their faces were masked; they were neither tall nor short, and they all wore miners' coats and hats and boots. Morgan pegged one of them as the leader though the man hardly spoke. No way to place him by his looks or the way he sounded.

Now they were close enough that Morgan could smell the whiskey stink. By the look of him, the one with the sawed-off was liquored up more than the others, but they'd all been drinking, and they all wanted to get first crack at the woman. Margaret Deakin knew what was coming, and she clutched at Morgan's arm, asking him to help her. He was saying something that meant nothing when the big man smashed him in the forehead with the butt of the shotgun, and he dropped like a stone.

He was facedown in the dirt, but he could hear what was happening. It seemed to be happening a long way off. Margaret Deakin was screaming. Nothing he could do about it. The screaming went on until it was stopped by something that sounded like a blow. Then he heard the leader's voice saying, "Hang him up on the gate." He felt himself being lifted, a rope biting into his ankle. He tried to kick out, but got kicked instead. Then he was hauled up high by the rope and left swinging by one foot in the dark. The sounds faded, and he blacked out.

Somebody splashed water in his face, and he woke up with a start that sent him swinging. Then he heard Margaret Deakin saying, "Wake up, Mr. Morgan. Please wake up. I'm going to cut you down. I can't loosen the rope. They broke my fingers. Get ready." The rope twanged as she cut into it. It was dark, and he couldn't see her. He couldn't see anything. The thick rope parted, and he fell hard in the dirt. He could see her shape bending over him, not much else. "Don't move, Mr. Morgan. Lay there a minute." Her voice sounded strange, and he knew in a fierce, blinding rage that the rotten, dirty, murdering bastards had punched her teeth out.

All he could do was lie there. "They've gone," she said in a despairing voice. He heard her spitting. She bent over him again. "I have to get you inside so you can lie down, blood is all over you. Can you get up?"

"I'm all right," he said. Sure he was. He sat up and untied the rope around his ankle, but when he tried to get up, his leg buckled under him. He came down hard on his ass and sat there trying to get his boot off. That took a while because the ankle was swollen and the leg was numb. He rubbed hard at the ankle, and the pain started as the blood began flowing freely. The pain was bad, but somehow he welcomed it, and used it to make himself stand up.

"I'm all right," he said again. Stamping his foot, trying to restore normal feeling, only made the pain worse. The hell with the pain! Some things were worse than pain. He should have done something before they got at the woman. He had a gun, and he should have used it. What they did to her was worse than a shotgun blast. And he had done nothing to stop it, just stood there and dropped his gun. . . .

He tried to tell himself that feeling badly about her was a waste of time. But the bad feeling was still there when they got inside the station, and he fumbled about until he found a lamp, put a match to it and saw how bad off she was. Her dress hung in tatters, and her thighs were stained with dried blood. One of her eyes was swollen shut, and her front teeth had been knocked out and blood still dribbled from her mouth. There were bite marks on her breasts, and some of her hair had been torn out.

He must have been staring at her harder than she could bear. "Please turn down the lamp," she said.

It took some coaxing, and a lot of firmness, to get her to lie down on the station keeper's dirty bed. He could walk now. Anyway, he could limp. There might be buggers in the bed; it was the only half-soft place he could put her. After what she'd been through, a few bedbugs didn't count for shit. She didn't want to look at him. "It won't do any good," she said when she heard him pouring water into a tin basin he had done his best to clean. But she didn't offer any protest when he found an old shears and cut the torn dress away from her body. He knew her torn bloomers would be somewhere outside in the dark.

She didn't move while he washed her with a fairly clean flour sack he had cut into squares. There was nothing to say so he didn't say it. Talking could wait until he got through cleaning her up. Or trying to. He changed the water twice before he finished washing her; then he went out to the coach and brought in her canvas grip and the lunch box. It looked like they'd driven off all the horses, so the next stage was the only way out of there. He could walk the twenty-five miles to the closest change station; no way she could walk any distance.

She stared at the roof while he looked in the grip for something to put on her. There were a few dresses, shifts, knee-length women's underpants, two pairs of low shoes, two towels, a cake of soap, a bottle of toilet water. Goddamn! he thought, looking at her few possessions.

He put clothes on her and placed a folded square of damp towel over her swollen eye. Nothing he could do about her broken mouth. He didn't try to brush her hair because patches had been torn out, and it would hurt like hell. All he could find to sit on was a three-legged stool. He put it beside the bed and sat on it, saying nothing. No point asking her how she felt. He knew how she felt.

"I wish I had something to drink," she said after he had been sitting there for awhile.

He held a mug of tepid water to her lips and she drank some of it. Then she pushed the mug way. "Can you find some spirits?" she said. "I would like something to drink."

"I'll see what I can do," he said, pretty sure he wasn't going to find any liquor in the luggage of the dead passengers. Outside it was still dark, but he could see better than before. The dead men's bags lay open beside the stage, their contents scattered all over the yard. He climbed up on the box to see if there might be a bottle hidden there. If there had been liquor there, the sons of bitches hadn't missed it. The dead men lay where they'd fallen. Their clothes had been ripped open in the search for money belts. The big man had killed them with a pistol so he wouldn't have shredded their wallets with a shotgun. Morgan felt nothing as he looked at them. Let the men on the next stage bury them if they wanted to take the time. It was none of his business.

Inside, while Margaret Deakin waited in silence, he searched for a bottle. Most station keepers were drinkers. There was sure to be a bottle someplace. He finally found it in a rickety lean-to that had been built onto the back of the one-room station. The bottle was less than half full, but it was more than enough. He wasn't going to let her have more than two drinks. There was nothing of the drinker about her, so that would be enough to put her to sleep. Bad whiskey or not, it would give her some relief.

Putting his arm around her, he raised her up so she could drink the whiskey and water he'd mixed in a tin mug. It wasn't all that strong, but her body shook as it burned her torn mouth and she gagged as it went down.

"Easy," he said, trying to take the mug away.

"No," she said, clutching it with the hand that wasn't broken. "Let me drink it."

What the hell. He let her drink the rest of the whiskey, then eased her head back on the stained pillow. Her eyes were closed, and he hoped she'd drift off to sleep without any more of the bad-smelling whiskey.

"I don't want to go on," she said without opening her eyes. Her voice was stronger than it had been. That would be the effect of the whiskey. "I can't face Llewellyn after what's happened. I feel dirty—dirty as the cheapest whore."

All Morgan could say was, "None of it was your fault. It had nothing to do with you."

Her face twisted into a bitter smile. "Llewellyn wouldn't understand that. He's a good man and he'd try to understand, but it would always be in his mind."

Llewellyn must be a real horse's ass, Morgan thought. "How could he blame you for what's happened? It's happened to other women, and their men didn't stop loving them."

It was getting cold, and he wished she'd go to sleep so he could cover her with a blanket. Then he could stretch out on the floor beside the bed and try to get some sleep himself. The pain from the crack on the head was so bad, it felt like he was dying. A big slug of whiskey would help the pain, but he wouldn't take it until she was asleep.

"You don't know Llewellyn," she said. "It would always be in his mind that I had done something to encourage those . . . those men. That's what they always think when a woman is . . ." Her face twisted into another smile so bitter that Morgan hated to see it. "Llewellyn has always wanted to marry a virgin, did you know that? Nothing else will do for him."

"Then don't tell him about the rape part," Morgan said. "You were beaten because you wouldn't give up your money, that's all." Morgan was warming up to this; it was a way out for her. "Listen to me. We'll take the next stage, tomorrow, so we'll be half a day late. I'll get off with you, a natural thing to be doing since you were beaten so badly. If your man, Llewellyn, isn't at the change station, we'll find him where he works. I'll tell him about the beating; then you tell him. Nothing else happened, you hear me? The other part doesn't have to come up."

"It won't work," she said, taking no time to think about it. "He'll know something happened, he isn't stupid, and I can't begin our marriage with a lie. Our plan was to be married the same day I arrived. How can we be married, the way I am? My face. My hair. My bosom. They bit me. I'm all bruised in my privates."

Morgan felt desperate trying to make it right for her. "Put him off for awhile, a week or two. After waiting for a year, what difference does a few weeks make?" Even as he said it, it sounded lame.

They had taken Morgan's silver watch, as well as his money and his gun. A battered tin alarm clock sitting on a nail keg said it was ten minutes to twelve. He must have been hanging from the swing gate for hours.

She turned her head and looked at him. "It's no good, Mr. Morgan, I'm going back to Yelverton. I don't know what Llewellyn will do, but I have to go back. Please give me another drink so I can sleep. I don't want to think about anything."

This time Morgan half filled the mug with whiskey, no water. "Take it slow; it's strong," he said, holding the mug to her mouth. He knew there was nothing he could say or do to change her mind. It was possible that time with her father would help her to get over this. Maybe she could even fix things up with this son-of-a-bitching Lllewellyn. Somehow he didn't think so. It was a goddamn fucking shame, the way things worked out for some people.

After she drank the whiskey, she lay back and seemed to relax. "I'll be right here," he said. A bullshit thing to say: how was he going to protect her if they did come back? He didn't have his knife or gun, and there were no guns around that he could find. He wondered where the station keeper was. Probably lying dead out back.

The next stage would be along in the morning, one of the long-distance stages that came from the east through Utah. It would be coming back from Carson City, and he'd ride with her to Yelverton, help her to get home. That would put another crimp into his plans, but Butterfield could wait. It looked like she was finally asleep. She didn't stir when he covered her with a blanket.

All he wanted was to stretch out on the floor, but he knew he ought to clean up. It wouldn't do her any good to wake up and see him looking like shit. A smoky mirror with a beer advertisement stenciled on it gave him a look at his face. There was a cut in his forehead and a lump the size of an egg. His face was caked with dried blood, and so was his hair. The shirt would have to be washed, but his pants were all right. He would look for his hat as soon as it got light.

It was one-thirty when he took a big slug of whiskey and lay down to sleep. Enough whiskey was left for her if she woke up and needed another drink. His shirt was steaming by the fire, and he was as clean as he was going to get. The whiskey didn't make him feel any better. What it did was knock him out. Later, when it was too late, he realized it was the head injury as much as the whiskey that put him into such a deep sleep.

Something woke him up, more a feeling than a sound. Margaret Deakin wasn't in the bed; the clock read three-forty-five; he'd been asleep for more than two hours. He called her name, but there was no answer. The door was still closed and barred so she hadn't gone outside. He didn't want to look in the lean-to, the only place she could be.

He found her. She was sitting against the wall of the lean-to with her throat cut, a straight razor gummy with soap and blood still in her hand. Her head hung forward. There was blood everywhere. Beside the body was the empty whiskey bottle.

Morgan knew he had to do something about this.

Lying on the bed, waiting for the hours to pass, he knew whatever he did would have to wait, just as burying her would have to wait, for the light. The self-hate and the wild anger were gone. Vowing vengeance was what an actor in a play did. It had no place in this dirty little house. Odd thing was, he thought later, he was able to get some sleep in spite of all.

The sun was full up by the time he got the grave dug and buried her. There was nothing to wrap her in but a dirty blanket, and he didn't want to use that. So he buried her as she was, didn't even cover her face before he put her in the grave and shoveled dirt on top of her. What difference did it make? He had to get her buried before she started to rot. No disrespect in thinking that. Just a fact of life.

After the grave was filled in, he covered it with rocks to keep the scavengers from digging in the night. He made no cross since her father could find the grave easily enough if he decided to hire an undertaker to move the body to Yelverton. He would write to her father when he got to Carson City, or Butterfield could do it.

Back in the station he made coffee and ate the rest of the sandwiches. What was that she'd said? "Please eat some sandwiches, Mr. Morgan. They'll go bad in the heat if somebody doesn't eat them." Something like that. Remembering it made him smile. It was too bad about Margaret Deakin, and that was the last grieving he'd do for her. From here on in he'd think of only one thing, and that was to kill the five men who had killed her. None was less guilty than the others. They all had to pay.

Digging the grave had left him weak and tired, the pain in his head still banging away, his hand shaking a little when he picked up the mug of coffee. The sandwiches hadn't gone bad, but they lay heavily on his stomach. It would take at least another day before he was feeling halfway normal.

It was no good, he decided, to leave the dead men as they were. The buzzards, already lighting down, would start tearing at the bodies if he didn't cover them. Last night that wouldn't have mattered, but now it did. He was beginning to think straight in spite of the skull-busting pain, and he had to make an effort to do the decent thing.

He covered the bodies with tarpaulins he'd found in the lean-to, then weighted them with rocks to keep the buzzards off. After that there was nothing to do but wait for the stage from McHargville. If the old clock wasn't haywire, it would be there in less than an hour. The buzzards knew he was in bad shape and kept flapping down from wherever they'd perched. He threw rocks and bits of wood at the filthy bastards, but they didn't go far.

He still didn't understand why they hadn't killed him. It was dark and maybe they fired a few shots at him before they lit out, but it was hard to think of the big man missing anything with that sawed-off. Maybe they missed because they'd had too much whiskey in them. Maybe they thought they heard something coming and ran like the cowardly bastards they were. Fuck it! He was alive and no matter how long it took he would make them sorry they hadn't finished the job.

The stage came and the bodies got buried. Two soldiers who were on the stage helped with the digging. Morgan told the driver some of what happened, but didn't get to finish it. The man kept saying, "Tell it to the law, mister. Tell it to Mr. Butterfield. I'm just a driver, see."

There were no fresh horses so the driver had to take it easy until they got to the next change station. The stage was hours late getting into Carson City.

Chapter Three

Butterfield was nowhere to be found in Carson City, a sprawling little village made up of a main building, coach barns, stables, repair shops, and corrals. The Nevada Stage Lines was out past the end of the town's commercial block and separated from it by a road. He didn't expect to find Butterfield working so late in the evening, but there was a chance he might be, the stage-line business being what it was. There were lights in the three-story main building, which had offices on the ground floor. When Morgan went in to ask about Butterfield, some clerk told him he'd probably quit for the day and gone upstairs to his living quarters. The clerk said he couldn't be sure because there was an outside staircase to the upper floors that couldn't be seen from his office. Mr. Butterfield might be taking a last look around before he went to bed. Morgan was welcome to look around himself.

He didn't do much looking. The two men he asked said he should try Butterfield's quarters or come back in the morning. While he was there a coach rolled in from somewhere, but he thought the whole place looked kind of dead and should have been a lot busier than it was. The repair shops were dark and no work was being done there. Usually work was being done at all hours of the night at the headquarters of a big line, and this could mean only two things: either the shopmen worked like demons and got their repairs done in the daylight hours, or Butterfield didn't have enough business or enough money to keep men working through the night. No hard-working demons around this place he decided on his way out. The Nevada Stage Lines operation had a general air of neglect, or failure, and the men he saw had the indifferent look of men who weren't sure they'd get their pay at the end of the week.

He didn't care a hell of lot how the business was going. If it hadn't been for Margaret Deakin, what he had to do about her, he would have been plenty sore after coming so far to tie in with a stage company that looked to be on the skids. But maybe he was wrong about that. Maybe old John Butterfield, said to be an invalid now, had come through with a big bank draft that would pump new life into the business. What the hell did it matter: he didn't know a thing about it. Unless William Butterfield was willing to wait, he wouldn't be bringing any horses down from Idaho. Anyway, not right off.

What he wanted to do was talk to Butterfield and learn all he could about these stage robbers. He still had Butterfield's letter folded in his hip pocket, not that it meant much now. Just the same, if he could get this other business over with, he'd be willing to make a deal with Butterfield, provided he talked straight and didn't try to fool around with the first payment. Going back past the main building he saw lights in what he took to be Butterfield's living quarters, but he didn't go up there. Morning was time enough. What he didn't understand was why Butterfield hadn't waited to hear what he had to tell. Maybe he had. Morgan knew he should have gone right to the stage depot instead of getting off in the middle of town to get a drink, then another and another. How much time he'd spent in the saloon he wasn't sure. He needed those drinks—the last drinking he'd have for a while—but he wasn't drunk. The hell with it! He'd get some sleep and talk to Butterfield in the morning.

To most men, renting a room in a whorehouse just to sleep wouldn't be such a good idea, a waste of money and cunt. Morgan knew better because he'd done it before, and though the price was a good bit higher than at a hotel, madams were often willing to come down in the price if it happened to be a slow night. Better to rent a room for some money than to have it go empty. This was Wednesday night—the dead middle of the week—and the miners who worked for the big companies, and that meant most of them, usually had no money for anything but food and tobacco. Saturday night was their night to howl, and the whorehouses, especially the quick-and-cheap places, got so busy the men had to stand in line.

Morgan had been in Carson City years before, and he knew of a house that was better than the quick poke emporiums. It might not be there any more, but he wanted to take a look. Tired as he was, it would have been simpler to go to a hotel instead of haggling with some madam, but he liked the idea of having women close by if he needed one during the night. Going to whorehouses to sleep hadn't always worked in the past. There were those times when he slept no more than an hour before waking up in the dark with a stiff cock and having to do something about it. Tonight would be different; it was a good bet he'd get a long, sound sleep in spite of having all those women so close. Could be he'd sleep even better than usual for having them so close. He liked the company of women and everything else they had to offer, and if it so happened that he couldn't get through the night without one, then so be it.

The house was the same, but the madam wasn't. Morgan remembered the madam from fourteen years earlier as a sweet-faced woman with a sour-looking bully to back her up. The madam he was talking to now wasn't half so sweet, and she didn't like the ugly lump on his forehead. Morgan forestalled her questions by telling about the bad fall he took when his horse spooked and threw him in a rocky place.

"Is that a fact?" she said, looking at him. "You're not a fighter, are you? I won't have men in here that start trouble."

"You'll get no trouble from me," Morgan said. "Like I told you, I just want to get a bed for the night. Get some sleep. I don't like hotels. I can pay if we agree on a price." And he showed her the wad of bills he got as change after he'd paid for his drinks with a fifty-dollar Mexican gold piece earlier that night. He had two more just like it hidden in the lining of his boot, and if there were times when he was forced to spend his emergency funds, he always put gold Mexicans back in his boot when he could afford it.

"No reflection on your ladies," he said before he started up the stairs to Room 7, "but I've got to get some sleep. If I find I do need one, I'll come to the head of the stairs and whistle."

The madam bridled at this suggestion. "You'll do no whistling in this establishment. Clap your hands like a gentleman. And don't you be thinking the young lady is included in the price of the bed."

Morgan was most of the way up the stairs when he heard the madam saying to the bully, "You meet all kinds in this business."

The room was all right. A table and chair, a double brass bed, a chamber pot under the bed, a framed copy of a painting of a girl picking flowers screwed to the wall. The sheets were clean and so was the room. He didn't try to hide his boots, but put them well under the bed. He left the paper money in his pants and hung them over the back of the chair with the rest of his clothes. There was no bolt on the door, but it didn't look like a place where customers got robbed after they'd fucked themselves to sleep.

He was asleep as soon as his head touched the pillow. At first there were bad dreams, and he woke up several times with sweat all over him. After that he slept soundly, no dreams at all, and it must have been hours later when the slight creak of the door opening awakened him, and he saw a woman standing there in the dim light of the turned-down lamp. She was young and fairly tall, with blond hair and light eyes, and had nothing on under the loose cotton dress that looked more like a nightgown than a dress, and even in the dim light he saw how good-looking she was.

"I thought I told the lady of the house," he began, without much conviction. The words trailed off as she came closer to the bed, her slippered feet hardly making a sound on the bare plank floor. Her breasts were big and firm and well-rounded and looked like they'd burst out of her dress at any moment. Morgan felt his cock stiffen.

"Mrs. Briggs doesn't know about this," she said in a low, musical voice like a lady singer talking. "She's been asleep for hours. I saw you from the parlor when you came in and you looked so battered and woebegone that I felt sorry for you. I'll be on duty till eight o'clock—it's five-fifteen now—and I thought I'd look in on you in case you needed anything. Something to eat? A bottle of beer? Mrs. Briggs doesn't allow hard liquor."

Morgan didn't believe any of it. If this house was like all the others, the girls got fed but didn't get paid unless they worked and got their cut of the bed money plus what tips they could wangle out of the customers. It was hard to think that a girl as good-looking as this would go a whole night without finding a pete, but there it was. Wednesday was a slow night, and maybe the few men who came in found her too refined. For some men fucking a refined woman was like fucking their sister, the schoolteacher, or the college-educated daughter of a bank president. They were so afraid they wouldn't get a bone on. Other men liked nothing better than to slam it into a woman who talked proper English and took a bath more than once a week. . . .

Morgan had no such peculiarities and he'd fuck anything that was halfway decent when he felt like it. Now, all of a sudden, he felt like it, and he held back the covers so she could get into bed. The flimsy dress dropped to the floor and she kicked it aside and was already reaching for his cock before he got the covers over her. It was all a show to make him horny, and he liked it fine. He liked women who put on a show, knew what they were doing, and gave a man his money's worth. This one was overdoing it a little, saying, "Oh your poor head," stroking his forehead with one hand while she stroked his cock with the other.

His head felt all right, no more pain, and his cock felt better than that. His cock was as stiff as a billy club, and he knew he was getting back to normal or was close to it. What he felt most of all was a sudden, desperate need for this woman, and though he hated to admit it, the thing back at the stage station had beaten him down, shaken his self-confidence, giving him bad dreams. He would have found it hard to explain why fucking this woman was so important, and then it came to him. He was alive when all the odds said he should be dead. As simple as that, and maybe a little crazy as well.

He turned her on her back and she opened her legs and he thrust into her all the way. Later there would be time for play acting, but for now he wanted to fuck her straight, plow her deep and solid, and then shoot his load. Needing her so bad, she might have been the first woman that ever lay down for him. It was good to feel his rigid cock shafting in and out of her, and his mind flashed back to the change station when, for an instant, death seemed so certain. He had faced death many times, but no matter how close it came, somehow there was always the feeling that it could be avoided.

His energy surprised her, and she laughed. "And I thought you were on your last legs," she said in that throaty voice. "Shows you how wrong you can be. The way you looked I thought to myself, that poor man needs a week in bed, headache powders, and chicken soup."

"No chicken soup," Morgan said. "Just you." And he drew it back and shoved it in right to the hilt. Her legs were wrapped around his back and her hot breath was in his ear. With his hands kneading her ass, she ground her crotch into his and used her cunt muscles like an expert, taking care not to seem too mechanical in her movements. A good whore tried to make a man believe that she was enjoying it, that he was different from all the other men she fucked. At any other time he would have enjoyed the make believe—it was part of the game—but right now he didn't care. It wouldn't have mattered if she just lay there and let him use her.

Usually he put some real skill—artistry, was that the word?—into his fucking. That was his way with a woman, except when he'd gone without a woman for a very long time. Like the other day when he came down from Idaho after nine womanless months and Marie, the Frinch whore who liked his thang, spread her legs for him. In he went like a pile driver, no artistry at all, and boy-o-boy did he need it bad. So much jism shot out of him when he came that it trickled down her thighs and wet the sheets. "Lord Almighty!" Marie had said. "You been buildin' up a real head a steam, ain't ye."

Marie was smart enough in her country way, but this one was smarter. "You're all tensed up," she said. "You're trying too hard. Let me help you to come, and then you'll be all right."

"I'm all right as I am," Morgan told her, not wanting to stop. His cock drove in and out like a piston, and her cunt was hot and tight and slick, but every time he came close to shooting his load nothing happened, and he had to go on pumping. His cock was still big and hard and he drove it with a fierce energy, but. . . .

"You're not all right," she said, pushing at his chest with both hands. "You're all tensed up. You have to let me help you." A strong shove got him off her and now she was on top and raising up to get his cock out of her. Then she moved down and took his cock in her mouth and began to suck it. His hands caressed her hair as she sucked him, and she didn't try to get too much cock into her mouth, just the head of it, and every time her tongue flicked across the head of his cock his balls tightened up so hard they ached. Now she was sucking him and moving her mouth up and down at the same down. Her hand reached up and grasped his cock just below the head, and she stroked him and sucked him at the same time. Morgan's ass kept raising up off the bed, and his hand closed over her hand and went up and down with it. He tightened his grip on her hand and moved it faster, and suddenly he started to come almost without knowing it. First there was a violent spurt that shot up into her mouth and she kept sucking the head of his cock as more and more jism rushed up from his balls. It was like he couldn't stop coming, and she kept on sucking and swallowing. There was a final surge, and then she pulled his cock out of her mouth and lay on top of him gasping for breath.

It took a while for him to stop shaking. Jesus Christ! he thought. He was grateful that she didn't ask if he felt better. Some whores, thinking of a big tip, pushed the love and kindness business too far. He felt drained and relaxed, and the next time he mounted her he'd be like he always was, glad to be in bed with a good-looking woman and thinking of the good things they were going to do together.

"Gracious!" she said, fondling his cock, "how can you get hard again so soon?" That was more of her playacting—

the compliment—and it made him smile.

"It's because I'm in bed with you," he said. A shitkicking thing to say but true enough: his cock wasn't quite as stiff as a ramrod, but it was getting there. He knew it would stand by itself even if she took away her hand.

"What do they call you?" he said. Earlier he wouldn't have cared if he never heard her name, and even now it wasn't important, but he thought he should ask, his way of telling her that to him she wasn't just a piece of meat.

"Amanda," she said. "My real name." The way she said it, Morgan knew it wasn't. "Aren't you going to ask what I'm doing in a place like this?"

"Well no," Morgan said. "I hadn't thought to ask you that. But now that you mention it, what are you doing in a place like this?"

"Sucking cocks, that's what I'm doing." She spat out the words like sour-apple pits. "So now you know."

Morgan tried to turn aside her bitterness with a joke. "I kind of suspected that," he said, regretting it the moment he said it. "But that's not fair," he blundered on like the shitkicker he was. "You asked me to ask."

"I'm sorry," she said in a sudden switch, sounding nervous. "Please don't complain to Mrs. Briggs about the way I talked. Men have complained about me, said I didn't laugh or smile enough or was too high-hat. God knows I've tried to be more jolly. You saw how I tried to cheer you up when I came in. But Mrs. Briggs doesn't like me to begin with. I'm here but I don't know how long I'll be staying. I don't know what I'll do if Mrs. Briggs kicks me out. I was in two other places before I came here."

"But what brought you here?" Morgan said.

"You really want to know? All right, I'll tell you. I thought we were well-off—my father was a cotton broker—but three years ago he was sent to jail for stealing from his company and we lost our house, we lost everything, and I had to find some way to make a living. I had some voice training so I tried to be a singer, but I wasn't good enough. I had belonged to an amateur theatrical group so I tried to be an actress. Nobody wanted me: I was stiff and awkward, and I couldn't remember my lines. I even tried to be a dancer, but it seems I have two left feet. I'll be honest with you, Mr. Morgan—what's the matter?"

"Just a cramp in my leg." He reached down to rub his leg. "Took a bad fall from a horse the day before yesterday. It's all right now." How the hell did she know his name? The only one he'd told it to was the clerk back at the stage office. It looked like somebody had followed him here—but who? Who would be interested enough to follow him or have him followed? It couldn't be one of the men from the change station. They could have killed him when they were there. It was something to think about.

"You were saying," he said.

"Oh yes. I was about to say I'd like to meet a rich man—preferably a *nice* rich man—and marry him."

"I hope you find him," Morgan said. She went on talking, but he heard only half of what she said. What he did hear he didn't believe—she sounded like a fanciful liar who made things up as she went along. But she was smart, and it was a good guess that Mrs. Briggs had sent her up to pump him for information. No, that couldn't be the way it was. She hadn't asked him a single important question. She could have heard his name downstairs. But why would Mrs. Briggs be talking about him, and who the hell was she talking to when his name was mentioned? It all brought him right back to where he started. Who was keeping track of his movements?

While she idly stroked his cock, Amanda was saying: "I'm afraid I'll never meet the right man in this place or any place like it. . . ."

The whole thing was a puzzle, Morgan thought, but he wasn't going to solve it so early in the morning, and in a whorehouse bed. The stores wouldn't be open yet—they had been closed when he got through drinking—and he wanted to buy a shirt and a hat before he went to see Butterfield. The shirt he had was stained and burned by lye soap and his hat had been carried away by the wind. More important than the hat and shirt was a gun. With somebody sneaking around behind his back, he sure as hell needed a gun.

"I might try San Francisco," Amanda was saying.

Still no questions. If she hadn't asked them by now, she wouldn't ask them at all. Morgan reached for her, thinking he'd have to pay for her, so why not make the most of it? His cock was hard, and he was ready to ride. This time the only tension was in his cock. He parted her legs and slid it into her in one smooth motion. Mrs. Briggs and her sneaky friend could go fuck themselves—he was having a good time.

But even as he larruped it into her, his mind kept going back to a faceless man who had followed him through the streets from Butterfield's. It would have been easy, the streets so crowded, the saloons open day and night, miners getting off their shifts, ore wagons blocking the intersections. The sneak could have killed him without much risk after he got away from the crowds and headed for this place. Carson City wasn't the wild lawless town it had been back in the Sixties, but even now gunshots in the night were no novelty. Best he could figure, the sneak had been sent out to keep an eye on him, no more than that. Whoever was behind it wanted to know where he went, what he did, and who he talked to. But why?

Damn! He wished he could keep his mind on his work. Amanda was looking up at him with a puzzled expression. After that he fucked her steadily and the puzzled look went away. "Nurse Amanda thinks you've made a full recovery," she whispered in his ear as he pulled his cockhead back to the edge of her cunt and buried it inside her with a long, smooth thrust. As soon as it was in all the way he let himself go, and he kept moving his cock while the jism shot out of it. And he kept on moving it even when there was nothing left to come. But all good things have an end, as the wise owl said, and it was with great reluctance that he finally pulled his cock out of her and wiped it with the damp sheet.

Amanda brought him a basin of warm, soapy water and a towel. Strong sun was coming through the paper window shade by the time he finished washing. The smell of soap reminded him of Margaret Deakin. She had been a very clean woman. Yes sir, so she had.

He kissed Amanda and gave her five dollars before he went down to pay Mrs. Briggs. It was money he could ill afford, but he felt he owed it to her for what she had done for him. A tough whore would have let him stew, might have laughed.

No one was hanging about when he went outside, unless it was the old man gimping along on one crutch, holding the handle of a beer bucket with the other. The street was quiet, mostly small houses, and there was nobody on it but the old man and down a ways two women gossiping.

Before he did anything else, he bought a pistol, a rifle, a knife, and boxes of shells. The man at the gun shop tried to sell him a new gunbelt and holster. He said he'd make do with what he had: a well-worn plain belt and holster of good quality leather, no cartridge loops. He was no gunman or lawman, and he didn't need all that shit. Anyway, you could reload just as fast with bullets carried loose in your pocket. The weapons he bought were secondhand, but in good condition, and the dealer let him go out behind the store and shoot at targets placed far back against a clay bank. Later he bought a watch that cost plenty.

He also bought a shirt and hat, then ate a big breakfast, and went to see Butterfield.

Chapter Four

"I think that's the last robbery we're going to see on my line," Butterfield said when Morgan finished talking.

"Why is that?" Morgan sat in a big oak chair with arms, and it creaked every time he moved. Butterfield was behind a big oak desk in an office with too much furniture. He was a short, slight man with ginger hair, a reddish face, and had a nervous way of talking. He'd offered Morgan a drink when he came in, and when Morgan said no thanks, he said he hardly ever drank himself. Morgan guessed he was forty or so.

Butterfield leaned forward, small in his big chair. "Have you ever heard of U.S. Marshal Jacob Van Wert? Jake, to friend and foe alike."

"I've heard of him." Morgan wished to hell Butterfield would get on with it. "The Terror of the West, the dime novels call him." Other names he'd heard were killer, backshooter, double-dealer, and perjurer, that was probably closest to the truth.

Butterfield leaned back in his chair, then changed his mind and leaned forward again. "A name and reputation well-earned. Jake Van Wert has been assigned to this case, with orders not to let up until the bandits are dead or behind bars. He's on his way, if he hasn't arrived already. My information is he'll be here either today or tomorrow. How do you like that?"

"Sounds like good news," Morgan said, not too interested in Van Wert. He wasn't going to leave the killers to Van Wert.

"Is that all you have to say?" Butterfield seemed a bit peeved.

"Why wasn't Van Wert here long before this?"

"Van Wert goes where they send him. I asked for Van Wert but didn't get him. Instead they sent a total incompetent who got his job through Republican politics. You see, I backed the wrong candidate in the last election for governor, but now we have a new president and a new governor, both good Democrats, and I'm finally getting some action. I'm a Democrat by conviction and, besides, it's good for business. Nevada is getting to be more and more of a Democrat state because of all the Irish miners here. Some of them can barely read, but they do love politics. Tammany arranges their naturalization papers an hour after they get off the boat."

Butterfield sure could run off at the mouth. "I guess you can tell Van Wert everything I've told you."

"Of course I can, but he'll want to talk to you. I would think you would want to talk to him. Jake Van Wert is a very famous man. Wherever he goes people want to shake his hand and buy him a drink."

Morgan didn't say he'd as soon kiss a rattlesnake as buy a drink for Van Wert. They hadn't gotten down to business yet, so why rile the man? "If he doesn't get here today our business will have to wait a while. I won't be here tomorrow."

"What? What are you saying?" Butterfield's ginger eyebrows shot up in surprise. "You just got here last night. First I waited in the office, then in my quarters, but you didn't show up. I know, I know, you told me the reason, but. . . ."

"I have to do something about Margaret Deakin." Butterfield gave a blank look and Morgan added, "the woman on the stage, the one they murdered." The little nervous man hadn't expressed much interest in Margaret Deakin, other than to say it was a shame, a terrible thing to happen. He'd sounded like a bored undertaker.

Butterfield didn't get it. "You mean you're going to try to track them down? For heaven's sake, Morgan, that's Van Wert's job. It's what he's getting paid to do, and he's very good at it, the best. Think what you're saying. You don't know what they look like, you say they were masked. You don't have a Chinaman's chance of catching them."

"I mean to kill them," Morgan said. "That's why our business will have to wait. I came here to tell you that. You'll probably want to reconsider some of the other bids."

"But I was counting on you. I thought we had a deal." Butterfield waved that aside. "You told me the woman killed herself with a razor."

Morgan said, "They murdered her as surely as if they'd used the razor themselves. I can't let them get away with it. I don't want to argue about it."

"Well I do." Butterfield pounded the desk with a small fist. "Business deal aside, I can't let you go off on a wild goose chase and get yourself killed. You're forgetting you don't even know what they look like and that they know you all too well. Leave it to Van Wert. What you're planning is foolish and dangerous. Another thing, Jake Van Wert has no use for vigilantes of any stripe."

Morgan started to get up and Butterfield said, "Have the courtesy to hear me out, sir. For the life of me I can't believe you're so headstrong as to throw away a business deal that should be profitable for both of us. We'll let that go for the moment, but we must get back to it. Tell me something. Perhaps I didn't take in all you said. Did you know this woman before you met her on the stage? Was she someone you knew from some other time in your life?"

Morgan said, "I met her that day for the first time. That's not the point."

"Then what is the point? I can understand your anger at what happened to her—I'm angry myself—but if she wasn't a relative, or an old friend, why are you so hell-bent on risking your life in this way? It doesn't make any sense."

"It makes sense to me. I don't expect you to understand."

"Of course I don't understand. I wish you'd explain it so I could. Will you let me talk! These men may not even be the same men who've been robbing my stages. In the past—bad as it was—they never killed anyone. It was always the passengers' money and valuables they were after, and the horses."

"That makes no difference to me." Morgan shifted in the creaky chair, wanting to get out of there.

Butterfield straightened his silk cravat, a nervous habit he had. "What I'm saying is this may be the work of drifters, outlaw scum drifting through on their way to California. God knows where they're headed. How on earth can you hope to find them?"

Morgan ignored that. "They wore miners' clothes. You said the men who committed the other robberies wore miners' clothes. It's the same gang all right, only this time they got drunk and went wild."

Butterfield wasn't ready to buy that cow. "Anybody can buy miners' clothes. There's a simple explanation. They'd heard about the other robbers wearing miners' clothes and decided to lay the blame on them by dressing the same."

"A lot of trouble to get so little. Ninety dollars from me, and the other passengers can't have had much."

"They got the mailbags, the horses. I'm telling you it's not the same gang. The other gang never killed anybody."

"I don't care," Morgan said. "I'll find them."

Butterfield was obstinate. "You can't know that. Be sensible, man. Honor your agreement with me. You'll benefit by it."

Morgan was thinking how much he needed the money. "We can still do business if you can wait a while."

Butterfield went to the window and waved his hand. "That's my business down there. It's still a sound business even with the railroads pushing through. We've got a Carson and Colorado depot right here in town. But the railroads don't go everywhere, maybe never will. So there's a lot of territory left for the stage business, a lot of money to be made."

Morgan said nothing. Booster talk; he wasn't interested.

"You could help me rebuild the business." Butterfield was back behind his desk. "Van Wert will stop the robberies, at least scare the thieves off for good. The McHargville division, all my divisions, will be free of trouble. They'd be fools not to quit it, and yet you ask me to wait. For how long? A month? Six months? A year? How do you know you won't get killed the first time you get close, if you ever do? These robberies have damaged my business, scared away passengers, and put my mail contract in jeopardy, but it's all going to stop."

"You have a lot of faith in Van Wert. He's only one man." Morgan didn't care what Van Wert did or didn't do. Butterfield could talk till he was blue in the face.

"He's the best there is. Damn it! Why can't you leave it to Van Wert? He'll either catch them or kill them."

Here we go again, Morgan thought. "They could get off if he brings them in. A smart lawyer could get them off.

I'd be the only witness. I'm ready to swear to anything, but it might not work. Even if they were found guilty they could get off with a life sentence."

Butterfield stared at him. "That isn't good enough for you?"

"Not by a long shot," Morgan said. "I would think you'd want to see them dead. It's your stage line they've been playing jakes with."

A stagecoach rumbled past the building, and it seemed to remind Butterfield that he was a serious businessman and that he should talk like one. "Putting them away for a very long time would satisfy me. I'm a businessman, and I can't afford to take these things personally. Every businessman has enemies, and they're not all stage robbers. If I flew into a blind rage every time I suffered some setback I wouldn't live to be fifty. You can see that, can't you?"

Morgan nodded. So much for Margaret Deakin. "I hear what you're saying, Mr. Butterfield." It seemed like Butterfield would say anything to hold him to the deal. He must want the Idaho horses pretty bad. Why couldn't he switch to one of the other bidders? "But I have to go ahead with this. Can you think of anybody that could be behind the robberies?"

Butterfield's ginger eyebrows shot up. "What are you saying? They're robbing stages on their own. I can't see that there's anyone behind it."

"I think different," Morgan said. "That business with the miners' clothes. Hard to identify men dressed like that. Somebody had to think it up."

"Why couldn't they think it up themselves? I once heard of bank robbers back in Pennsylvania that dressed as Amish farmers."

Morgan said, "I'm not asking you to accuse anybody. I'm just asking for a name, somebody who might have an interest in wrecking your stage line. Surely you've thought about that?"

Butterfield took time to think. "I have and I haven't. If there is somebody like that, why haven't his men burned my coaches and stations? Stations can be rebuilt for next to nothing, but coaches cost more money than you can imagine."

Morgan wondered if Butterfield ever got any of his horses back. It was not unknown for businessmen to make deals with kidnapers and thieves through a third party, but most were too ashamed or embarrassed to admit it. He let the question go.

"They wouldn't burn your coaches if they planned to buy you out." Morgan pushed a little harder. "I could start asking questions all over, but you'd know better than anybody. I need a name. Word of honor, you won't be connected with anything I do."

Butterfield did some more thinking, then he said, "The only name I can think of is Niven Menzies. He runs a mud wagon line out of Silver City. That's a good ninety miles from here. You passed through it on the stage."

Morgan half remembered the name being called out. He must have been sleeping soundly.

Butterfield went on. "Menzies runs his line to remote mining camps. Roads are too bad to take regular coaches, so he uses mud wagons and mules like they all do. I guess you know that."

"Does he have enough money to buy a regular stage line?"

Butterfield considered the question. "I would say he does. There's money in the mud wagon business if you can get enough passengers. Menzies does, and he operates a freight line as well. Yes he's got money and could get backing I would think, if he needed it. After all, he's a Scotchman."

A Scotchman! Morgan didn't ask if Menzies was a big man, or if he had a Scotch accent. He wasn't going to share his hard information with anybody unless he had to.

Butterfield answered the question he didn't ask. "I don't know if he was born in Scotland or not, but I have heard he takes great pride in being Scotch, why I can't imagine. I never met the man, just know him by name and reputation."

"He has a bad reputation?"

"I didn't say that. I never heard of him doing anything in Nevada, but he did serve an eight-year sentence for manslaughter in New York. A fellow jailbird spotted him out here. They call him Sing-Sing Menzies behind his back. You want to know if he tried to buy me out. No, he didn't, but I heard he was making inquiries into my financial position."

"How long ago was that?"

"A few months after the robberies began." Butterfield fiddled with a pencil on his desk. "I see what you're getting at, but I'm making no accusations, mind you. I don't want any trouble with Menzies."

"Does your father know about these robberies?" Morgan knew he was stepping over the line here.

The pencil Butterfield was fooling with snapped in two, and he tossed it into a wastebasket. "That's a personal question, but under the circumstances I'll answer it. I'm the general manager of this line, but my father owns it. Of course, he knows. He insists on knowing everything, good or bad. Needless to say, he isn't happy with the way things have been going. If you're asking why he doesn't put more money into the line, the answer is he has no intention of investing a single additional penny. 'Not one red cent,' as he put it in a recent letter, and there was more about throwing good money down a sinkhole. More than once he's hinted that it might be better if he were to sell the line, to take what he could get for it, and I went to work for a friend of his who owns a sheet-metal factory in St. Louis. That's where my father lives."

"A far cry from stagecoaching," Morgan said.

"Well you might say that," Butterfield said with a mild show of anger. "But I swear, nobody's going to drive me out of the stage-line business. I'm going to make a go of it, in spite of the reverses I've suffered, yes, and in spite of my father. Don't be surprised. He's old and sick, has a heavy hand, but we get along most of the time."

Morgan stood up. "Good luck to you. I have a last favor to ask: can you tell me where I can buy a good horse? I don't want to waste time going from one stable to another."

Butterfield stayed behind his desk. "Yes, I can do that. Go to Muller's Livery on Walker Street—wait, I'll give you a note—and he'll fix you up. I'm sorry we couldn't do business, but you understand I'll have to make other arrangements. Take care of yourself."

Morgan was at the door when Butterfield said, "Where will you be if Van Wert wants to know?"

"I don't know. Maybe taking a tour of the town. I have to start somewhere. I could be on my way to Silver City if I happen to find the right horse." That, Morgan thought, was no less than the truth.

"Van Wert won't like that," Butterfield called out across the big room. "It's too vague."

"Van Wert can go to hell!" Morgan said, and closed the door behind him.

Muller's was no distance, but he had to go through the busiest part of town to get there. Lord, but it was a crowded town, the miners working for wages, the would-be independent miners still drifting in twenty-five years after the first big strike, the usual hangers-on sniffing out easier money: cardsharps, phony stock peddlers, small-time thieves. He didn't think he'd been followed to or from Butterfield's, but there was no way to be sure. With the buying and testing of the guns, the other things, including the talk with Butterfield—at least he had a name—it was one-thirty when he turned onto Walker Street.

Muller, an oldish peg-legged man with a prophet's beard, read Butterfield's note and put it in his pocket. "Be proud to fix up any friend of Mr. Butterfield, to give a good deal like he asks, only I ain't got the right horse. Most my business is in wagon horses. What saddle horses I got will not do for a good friend of Mr. William Butterfield. Got some good geldings coming in this evening, or so I'm promised. You want to ask around—go to the other stables—or wait a bit? Can give you a good horse at a good price, if you want to wait. Nine o'clock this evening, roughly about that time."

"I'll wait," Morgan said. "What kind of money would you have in mind?"

"Saddle horses come high in Carson. Everything comes high in Carson," the stableman said. "But don't you fret the price. Mr. Butterfield says to make you a good deal, and that's what you'll get."

Morgan left it at that. If Butterfield had that much drag with Muller, then at least he'd get a good to middling horse. Muller hadn't guaranteed a fiery steed for fifty dollars, and that was all to the good. He would have gone elsewhere if he had. He could have gone looking but didn't feel like it. Trying to buy a horse in a hustling, money-hungry town like Carson would likely be a bother, and even if he said he was in the horse business and knew horses up and down, out would come the nags with ginger up their asses to make them prance, and one and all they'd be guaranteed to be as tough and smart as mules, as sweet natured as lambs, as fast as racehorses. For now, Muller looked to be his best bet.

Just the same, waiting from two o'clock till nine left a big hole in his day. He wanted to get to Silver City to see what this Niven Menzies, otherwise known as Sing-Sing Menzies, looked like. Maybe he'd made a mistake in not asking more about Menzies, who could be a small old man of seventy for all he knew. The fact that he'd served eight years for manslaughter didn't mean much. Manslaughter might be a serious crime back in New York, but here in Nevada it didn't get that much attention from the law unless the man you killed was well liked, a veteran of the War of 1812, or happened to be free with the drinks.

But Menzies was the only name he had, Morgan thought, walking up from Walker Street to the main drag. Small and old and seventy though he might be, he had been asking about Butterfield's "financial position"—so Butterfield had said—and he warranted a look-see even if it came to nothing. For the moment though seven hours stretched ahead of him, and all his looking would have to be done in Carson.

The needle in the haystack, he thought, standing still a minute. The hell of it was the murdering bastards could be anywhere, right here in Carson, or a hundred, or two-hundred miles away, and with news of the famous man catcher Van Wert flashing over the telegraph, they could have split up and gone their separate ways.

Gambling halls and saloons were the best places to look. Men who stole for a living usually liked to drink and gamble and whore. The whorehouses would have to wait because it took money just to get inside them. His money was going fast, and he still had to buy a horse, a saddle, and supplies. And he couldn't dawdle in gambling halls too long without gambling or they'd show him the door.

Saloons it had to be, and he didn't look forward to it. Saloons were all right for a few beers or a long awaited bender. Otherwise you got sick of the noise, the dumb talk and the loud music. But there it was. You sure as hell couldn't stop people in the street and ask, "Excuse me, sir, but would you happen to have seen a fella with jug ears and little oval eyeglasses? He's my cousin Jethro, and I'm looking all over for the rascal." At least one answer would be: "Why don't you quit this panhandling and go to work, big strong fella like you?"

He bought his first beer in The Pearl Of The West and took his time drinking it. It was crowded to the doors, like every saloon in Carson, the drinkers five deep at the bar, a mechanical piano rattling away in back. Asking after Jethro was easier in a saloon: somebody was always asking after somebody in a saloon. But nobody had seen the rascal. Jethro himself wasn't there, with or without the odd-shaped eyeglasses. A few men had jug-handle ears, but none of them was Jethro.

All he drank was half a mug of beer. Beer was fine for killing thirst, no more than that. He wasn't about to drink till he was sloshed. The next place he poked around in was pretty much the same. Smelly, noisy, crowded. It was after three when he went to the third place; his watch read four-twenty when he left the fourth.

Between the fourth and the fifth he ate a sandwich and drank a lot of coffee. Four mugs of beer could make you dull headed, if not drunk, and that's how he felt. Not tired, just dull. Maybe he was wasting his time, but what the hell else was there to do till nine o'clock, roughly that time, the stablekeeper had said. It could be a lot later.

Saloons five and six didn't turn up anything either. It was eight-fifteen and getting dark when he pushed his way into what he'd decided would be the last place that day. If nothing happened there, he'd go back to the stable.

This saloon wasn't as crowded as the others, and he understood why after he tasted the beer. Most Carson beer was only fair to middling. This was downright bad, as if they'd made it in the cellar and washed their socks in it before it was barreled. There was room at the bar, and he found himself standing beside a man holding a beer mug with an inch of beer at the bottom of it. The mug was on the bar, and the man was holding the handle as if to keep the bartender from taking it away.

Morgan knew a freeloader when he saw one, but he asked if by any chance he'd seen Cousin Jethro. Once again Jethro was described, the jug ears, the eyeglasses. "Thought you might have noticed the eyeglasses," Morgan said. "Don't see many like them."

The way he was dressed made it hard to tell what he did for a living. Wool shirt, leather vest, miner's canvas pants, scuffed army boots. His big hat was creased in the back, Montana style. His long, thin stubbled face was caved in over empty gums, though he still had some of his front teeth.

"You see a few," he said, licking his lips, swirling the dregs of his beer. "Maybe I did see a fella like you described. You see so many people it's hard to remember this one from that one. I got to think a minute."

"Be obliged if you would."

"I'm thinking, mister," the man said irritably.

Morgan drank his beer, then pointed at the man's nearly empty mug. These bastards could be tetchy: best to ask.

"I won't say no to that," the man said, watching the bartender pull his beer. "What name does this cousin of yours go by?"

"Jethro, like I said. Jethro Gilmore."

"I'm Roy Smeal. You'd be?"

"Grady Armstrong," Morgan said.

They shook hands and he bought the freeloader another beer. There was every reason to believe that this beer-beggar was just stringing him along, but what the hell: something might come of it. One or two more beers—if nothing then—he'd go to see Muller. He signaled for another beer. The moocher sure put it away.

"It could mean a few dollars if you could remember a little faster," Morgan said. "Don't mean to rush you but . . ."

"How much is a few dollars?" the man said quickly.

"Five dollars. Can't spare much more than that."

"I could remember better with the five in my hand."

"No hard feelings, but I can't do it. Short on money as it is. Be seeing you. Got business to attend to."

The freeloader looked at his mug, then at Morgan. "Tell

you what, mister, you come back in an hour, and maybe I'll have something for you. Fair enough?"

Morgan nodded and went out. It was full dark now, and he stood behind a wagon until the freeloader left the saloon a few minutes later. Then he followed him.

Chapter Five

Morgan had left change on the bar, enough for a few more beers, and if the moocher wasn't rushing out to find a better tasting brand, he was making tracks for somewhere else. Whatever it was, he was moving right along, shoving his way through the sidewalk crowds, dodging the wagon traffic in the streets. Morgan had to walk fast to keep up with him, not so easy in the busy streets, harder when the streets got quiet. The only thing that helped was the man didn't look back even once.

For a while the rummy's boots sounded loud on the hollow boardwalks. Morgan couldn't understand why the rummy didn't hear him coming along behind. If he did hear he gave no sign of it, didn't even turn his head, or try to dodge off in the dark. There were no businesses this far out, more shacks than houses, no boardwalks, no street lights. Morgan passed a run-down little grocery store, but it was closed. A few of the shacks and houses showed lights, not many.

The baked-mud street came to an end, but the rummy kept going. It was dark out there, and the only light was reflected light from the town. Morgan could see the rummy moving ahead of him, but where in hell was he going? Maybe he lived in the town dump. Maybe he was rushing home to put the baby rats to bed. Morgan thought he saw a light and followed the rummy across a dry wash before he could see it plainly. The rummy ran on to a house where light showed from one window. By its shape and size it was a small two- or three-room house, not a shack. The rummy went in and the door banged behind him, cutting off the light. There was no dog or it would have barked. Morgan moved closer.

Through the torn shade Morgan saw the rummy talking to the jug-eared man. Yes sir, there he was, but he wasn't wearing his eyeglasses. Morgan's hand dropped to his gun without thinking, and he knew he had to get a hold of himself. It would be so easy to drop the son of a bitch where he stood. But that wasn't the way to do it. The killing would have to wait till after the bastard talked his head off, told everything he knew, and all the time begging for his life. That would be the good part, Morgan thought, to have the woman-killer down on his knees, pissing and shitting in his pants, crying for mercy. . . .

The hell with that! Make him talk, kill him quick, Morgan told himself, but even as he thought about it he knew it might be altogether different when the killing time came. If he couldn't control himself by then it would be very bad for the man with the jug ears. So what, he thought. Kill him any way that makes you feel better.

He couldn't hear all that they were saying. The two men were over by the fireplace; a table with cups and plates on it was between them. On the fire a kettle was whistling and neither of them moved it away from the heat. Morgan heard his name a few times, other things he couldn't make sense of. None of it mattered: he'd make the fucker sing louder than the kettle when it was time.

The kettle went on whistling while the jug-eared man dug into his pocket and gave the rummy bills and coins. Morgan ducked down as the rummy came out and headed back toward town, moving fast. Morgan looked in the window just as the jug-eared man kicked the whistling kettle off the fire. The kettle hit the side of the fireplace and the jug-eared man screamed as the scalding water splashed him on the legs. He was still cursing and feeling his legs when Morgan came in through the door.

Morgan held his gun steady and reached around behind him to lock the door. The only sound was the fire still hissing. "What's your name?" Morgan said. "Say it straight out, or I'll shoot the legs from under you."

"Tobias Canty. Tobe Canty. Who are you? What do you want? If you're fixing to rob me there's nothing here worth taking." Without the eyeglasses and the bandanna, Canty looked younger than Morgan had figured, no more than twenty-five, and the voice, what Morgan remembered about it, was the same. He could see all right without the specs, no squinting, not a bit.

Canty had some nerve, but it would go fast, Morgan knew. Few men—and surely not this man—could stand up to what he'd do if he could. But nothing had happened yet, so Canty was hangdog defiant, or trying to be.

"I don't know you. Who are you? This is crazy." The words came out fast, but trailed off on crazy. He took a deep breath and tried again. "What can you have against me? I never saw you before in my life."

Morgan swung a chair away from the table and set it down in the middle of the room. "Sit," he said. No rope was in sight, but there was a ball of twine in a corner. It would have to do. He threw it close to the chair and told Canty to tie his feet to the legs. He didn't think Canty was much of a threat, but he didn't want to have to lay him out—maybe kill him—should he try something. Thinking of Margaret Deakin, it wouldn't take much to make him kill this man.

Canty reached down to tie his feet, saying over and over, "This is crazy. This is crazy." After his feet were tied Morgan got behind him, jerked him back and tied his hands to the chair, though he hated to touch the slimy bastard. Canty was still talking by the time he finished.

Morgan didn't slap his mouth shut. Instead he got another chair and sat on it, leaning forward. "I want the names of the men who were with you when you robbed the stage and raped the woman. The woman is dead now. She cut her throat out of shame. She killed herself, but you and the others made her do it. That woman—I want you to know—was a good friend of mine, and you raped and murdered her. I could use a knife or a hot poker, but I'd as soon not. Now think on what I've said, and tell me what I want to know."

Morgan found himself listening to his own voice, as if it belonged to somebody else. He hoped it sounded reasonable—that was the commonsense side of him. The other side of him wanted to get right down to the knife and the red-hot poker. But for now—as long as it lasted—he had himself under control. What he feared most—you couldn't make a dead man talk—was what he'd do to Canty if his hate and anger broke loose.

"Last chance," he said quietly. "Tell me what I want to know."

"I don't know what you're talking about," Canty said again. "I never robbed any stagecoach, and who is this woman you're talking about? I'm telling you, you've got the wrong man, whoever you are. Do I look like a stage robber? I've got friends in Carson—ask them."

Morgan drew his knife and Canty tried to look away from it. "I don't have much time, so listen good. I can castrate you, cut out your eyes, or make you deaf and dumb with this. I can fix your legs so you'll never walk again." Canty's eyes crossed as Morgan touched the bridge of his nose with the point of the knife. No blood came. Morgan's voice remained steady, quieter than it had been. "You'll feel pain like you never imagined, pain so bad you'll beg me to kill you. But I won't kill you, and you won't die of the pain. You don't want to go through that, so tell me before it starts." Morgan dropped his voice to a whisper. "After what you did to that woman, I don't know that I'll want to stop."

Canty licked his lips and stared at the knife. "You'll kill me anyway. You want to kill me."

"I want to kill you, but I won't unless you—" Morgan let a few seconds go by. "Talk straight; then I'll give you to the law, let the law deal with you. What you tell me will get you hung or get you life—that's good enough for me. Either way you'll murder no more women."

"Why don't you hand me over right now," Canty said, seeing a way out of this. "Let the law deal with me, like you say."

Morgan wanted to spit in his face. The shifty bastard was figuring that once he was inside the safety of a jail he could deny everything, tell how he was threatened and beaten by this crazy man, and then send for a lawyer. Morgan knew he'd get a good one too because the man behind the gang would want him to have the best available law-talker.

"I want to hear it from you," Morgan said. "I'm getting impatient, Tobe. The names of the four other men, what they look like, where they can be found. The name of the man behind the robberies—everything. Don't make me start on you, Tobe."

Morgan still had the knife in his hand. He didn't know how much cutting he'd do on Canty if he had to. He knew he'd do some.

"All right," Canty said at last.

"Start with the man who gave the orders."

Canty said, "I only know him as Boss. We all had made-up names, his idea. In order to keep one man from turning on the others, selling them out for a reward, informing to the law if he got caught. So he was Boss, and I was Specs, and the others were Bear and Little Bear and Gent. Bear and Little Bear look like father and son, but I don't know where you can find them. Or anybody else. We met up for the robberies, then went our different ways."

Morgan turned the point of the knife. "I swear," Canty said.

Morgan didn't know how much of it was true. Other gangs worked like that—a few did anyway—so why not this gang? The thing was, Canty could say anything he liked, his descriptions of the four other men as phony as stock certificates with the ink still wet. If he thought he could weasel out of this with some fanciful story—Morgan thought of Amanda the liar—he was dead wrong. Dead wrong and soon to be cold dead. Morgan meant to kill him no matter what he said, but Canty didn't know that.

"Boss named you Specs because of the eyeglasses?" Morgan said. "So the people you robbed would remember the eyeglasses and forget about the jug ears?"

"That's right. I just use them for reading, never wear them out of the house. On our first job Boss spotted them in my shirt pocket and told me to put them on. That's how I got to be Specs."

Boss was a right smart fella, Morgan thought, that is, if Canty himself wasn't the so-called brains behind this grubby outfit. Canty read. Books were stacked on the dresser that Morgan had pushed in front of the torn window shade. But that didn't mean a thing: anybody could have planned what they'd been doing.

"You say Bear and Little Bear look like father and son. Bear was the big man with the sawed-off, the one that dropped me. Nobody else was that big."

Canty said, "Bear's son is big but nowhere as big as his father. The resemblance is in the face, the shape of the face. They have the same small eyes set back in their heads. And the same stiff black hair standing up wild."

"Bear was gray around the ears," Morgan said, not moving the knife. No good making the fucker too nervous. For what it was worth, he was talking right along.

Canty looked at the knife. "Bear is gray at the sides and has gray streaks on top. But his hair is thick and wild like his son's. That's the best description I can give you. I swear it. Can I have a drink of water?"

"Not till we're finished." Canty wouldn't need water—wouldn't need anything—by then. "Think hard, Tobe. What do you think the big man and his son do for a living? When they aren't robbing stages? Ranching, farming, mine work?"

"I don't know what they do, no more than I know what Boss and Gent do. They could work at different things like I do. Why can't you give me some water? I'd talk better if I had some water."

"You'll talk anyway," Morgan said. "You'll get all the water you want before you go to jail." It was time to move on. "Gent got his name because he has gentlemanly ways, is that right?"

"He tries to talk like that, but he's a phony." Specs doesn't like Gent, Morgan thought. Canty added, "If he's such a gentleman what's he doing robbing stages, fancy talk and all?"

"I'm surprised Boss let him talk so much."

"Boss didn't like any of us to talk more than we had to. No need to tell us that. Nobody wanted to talk, only Gent did. Boss used to tell him to shut up."

"Describe him. Make it quick." Morgan knew he had to move this along. It had been about eight-forty-five when he left the saloon. If he didn't show up by ten, or thereabouts, the rummy might come back here. He didn't want to kill a goddamn rummy. Anyway, it might not be the rummy that showed up.

Canty said, "He's about five-eight, long face kind of pale, dark eyes, in his forties. Dark hair, a waxed mustache, kind of. I mean, he puts wax on it to make it look fuller. I don't know what he does. He's got soft hands, like maybe he's a gambler or a barber, some trade that don't get his hands dirty. Maybe a storekeeper or an undertaker."

Now for Boss, Morgan thought. He should have started with Boss, though he was pretty sure he wasn't the one that sat home safely and did the planning. But that was just a guess. It didn't have to go beyond Boss.

"What does Boss look like?" Morgan said, not sure that all he was hearing wasn't a pack of lies. Canty was talking his head off, or so it seemed, but Morgan remembered what a Kansas City police detective once told him: "Sometimes when they start to talk it's hard to stop them, especially when they're lying or only telling part of the truth. Doesn't happen every time, but it does happen. You have to use your own judgment as to what's worthwhile."

"Describe Boss," Morgan repeated.

"He's like every fella you ever saw," Canty said. "Five-ten or so, brown hair I guess, not bad looking, not good looking either. Had a mustache on one job, didn't have it on the others, a full face. I don't know what he does—that's the truth. All I know about him is he knew the robberies he wanted to pull and sent us a letter saying where and when. Always about a week ahead. Enough time to get there."

Morgan checked his watch. Ten past ten. Shit! "Where were they postmarked?"

"Different places. McHargville, Silver City, Edgeworth, other places I can't recall. Maybe I could if I had time."

"Forget that. Did Boss recruit you himself?"

"Here in Carson, in a saloon. Got talking at the bar, talked some more at a table. How would I like to make some money, so on. Boss knew I'd been turned down for a job at Butterfield's. I asked him how he knew. Told me he knew, that's all. Said robbing his stages was a way to get back at Butterfield. No big risk. I was broke, so I agreed to come in. Boss said I'd be hearing from him. Only half believed it, but I did."

That would have to do. "I'm going to cut you loose now," Morgan said. "Then you're going to jail. Any tricks I'll shoot you dead."

Morgan meant to use the knife. Even out here a gun made too much noise. A knife made no sound, neither could Canty. He would set the house afire with the lamp.

Canty stood up rubbing his wrists. For a man who thought jail was next he perked up fast. "Yes sir, no tricks—you got the gun. Can I have a drink of water now?"

"Make it quick." Morgan thought he heard something. The wind had picked up and the roof creaked. The hell with that—get it done. Canty was still drinking, his back turned, when a boot or a fist hit the door. Canty spun around and Morgan shot him through the heart. He was still falling when a shotgun blast blew the door open. It hung by one hinge. Somebody shouted, "Throw the gun out, Morgan. This is Marshal Malley. Do it quick. This is the law. You hear me? Come out with your hands up."

Morgan went out and saw the rummy hiding behind three men with badges. One had a shotgun. No need to guess who the marshal was. Malley was wide and big, crowding sixty, wore a gray suit and a gray derby, had a well-combed handlebar mustache, and carried a short barreled Sheriff's Model Colt .45. The mark of the lawman-politician was stamped all over his beef-fed face.

"Stand as you are," he said, "while we take a look at you."

From behind him the rummy said, "That's the man. Said his name was Grady Armstrong, but it's Morgan. Tobe told me. I told you he was going to kill Tobe."

"So you did, Roy," Malley said. "Don't tell me again. Let's go and see how Tobe is doing—not you, Roy. Take yourself off." Malley fished a fifty-cent piece out of his vest pocket and flipped it to the rummy. "You go first, Morgan."

One of the deputies was down on one knee beside the dead man. "He's dead all right," the deputy said.

"I have eyes in my head," Malley said, no sharpness in his voice. "You fellas look around in the other rooms, see what you can turn up. Find any evidence bring it out and lay it on that table. *All* the evidence, don't you know." Now there was a rasp in his voice.

He holstered the short Colt, but stayed back from Morgan. "Now sir, what is this all about?"

Morgan told him. The killing of the guards and the passengers, the rape and beating of Margaret Deakin, what happened to himself. "The woman was so shamed she killed herself—cut her throat with a razor—during the night."

"Why didn't they kill you?" In the other rooms the deputies were turning the place upside down.

"I don't know."

"All this is news to me. Just as well: my jurisdiction doesn't extend beyond the city limits. This man you killed lived just inside the line, so that makes it my business. Why did you kill him? You had the gun and the knife."

"He jumped me when you banged on the door. I don't know who he thought was out there, but he grabbed a chair and tried to brain me. I had to shoot him."

"Sure you did," Malley said, looking at a chair that Canty's falling body had overturned. "But he talked—told you a lot—before you had to kill him."

Morgan said, "He told me some things. I don't know how much of it was lies. If you hadn't barged in I might have got some truth out of him."

Malley didn't mind the barging in remark, and he didn't seem too interested in what Canty might have said. "It's a good thing for you there are no marks on his face. Otherwise, I'd have to suspect you'd been beating him up. You're going after the rest of these bandits, are you?"

"I mean to."

"Is it possible that Butterfield didn't tell you about Van Wert, the scourge of badmen everywhere?"

"He told me," Morgan said. The deputies were bringing things in and spreading them on the table. One of them was Margaret Deakin's lapel watch. Morgan pointed to it and said what it was. "There's an inscription inside the lid. To Margaret, with deep affection, Llewellyn. See for yourself."

Malley looked at the watch. "Looks like Tobe was there all right, not that I doubted you for a minute. Is that all the money you found?" he said to one of the deputies. On the table were wallets, rings, snuffboxes, guns, a small stack of money held together by a rubber band.

"We're still searching," the deputy said.

Malley grunted. "Van Wert's been looking for you," he said to Morgan. "Beats me why they transferred Jackson and put Van Wert in his place. A fine man, Jackson, smart, determined, good at his job."

"Butterfield says he didn't know what he was doing."

"Poppycock! Jackson's as good as they come. We didn't trade information—federal and local lawmen don't get on—but I respected him. I wish I could say the same for Van Wert. Oh well, it's not for me to be downgrading a fellow officer."

"I'll talk to him when the time comes," Morgan said.

"Why do I have the feeling you don't want to?"

"He'll warn me to keep out of this."

"To put it mildly," Malley said. "He'll warn you with his fists if there's nobody around. There's only one hero in every piece he appears in, and that's himself. Have as little to do with him as you can."

"Then you're not arresting me?"

One of the deputies came in and put a big gold watch on the table. "Solid gold but it don't run," he said.

"No reason to arrest you," Malley said. "All this property Tobe helped to steal, the dead lady's watch, and so forth. Speaks for itself. Self-defense while trying to make a citizen's arrest, is how I see it. Coroner's jury could have other ideas, though I doubt it. Inquest ten o'clock tomorrow morning. Don't disappoint us."

Morgan got his knife and gun back. "That money there," he said, meaning the bills on the table, "ninety dollars of it belongs to me."

"Everything on that table is evidence, including the money. It has to be held, don't you know. That's the law, son."

Morgan, in his late thirties, was now son. "Then I don't get it back?"

"Not right this very minute," Malley said. "What you can do is put in a claim, in writing, with a list of the serial numbers. I'll see what I can do to hurry it through."

Morgan knew he was being warned not to press his claim. "Good-night, Marshal," he said.

Chapter Six

Morgan bought a pretty good horse and asked Muller if he could spend the rest of the night in the stable. It was late to be going to a hotel, and he had to be up early. Muller, who slept there himself, found nothing unusual in this and wouldn't think of taking money for a few hours sleep on a cot. The gelding cost less than he thought it would, and he didn't know why. Any friend of Mr. Butterfield, et cetera. Muller winked when he said it. What the hell did that mean?

When Morgan had gotten there the night before, it was after midnight and Muller was still waiting for the horses to arrive, from where he didn't say. Morgan thought it was an odd hour to be bringing in horses. A lot went on in Carson. None of his business.

Van Wert had been looking for him, Muller said. Came twice, left the same message both times: come see him at the Carson Hotel, and don't dally on the way. "Words of that nature," Muller said.

Now it was morning, and he was climbing the courthouse steps, ready to start for Silver City as soon as the inquest was over. A quick verdict of justifiable homicide, Malley seemed to think. Not much chance of ducking Van Wert, better to get it over with.

The inquest was held in the regular courtroom, high ceilinged, wood paneled, and dusty. Morgan and Malley and Roy the rummy were the only witnesses called. There was a fair crowd. Butterfield was among the spectators. So was a man Morgan took to be Van Wert. Morgan had no idea how old Van Wert was, but he expected him to be older than he looked. Lean faced and lanky, bare faced and blue eyed, he looked to be no more than thirty-five in spite of his dry, thinning hair. There was a stillness, almost a mildness about him that belied his fearsome repution, but with or without the badge he looked like the law.

Malley, the first to take the stand, said Tobias Canty was about thirty years of age, a native of Michigan or Illinois, he couldn't be sure, and had been in Carson City for two or three years. Questioned by the coroner, who treated the city marshal with elaborate courtesy, Malley said Canty had worked at any number of jobs: handyman, store clerk, stableboy, even company miner for a few weeks. In his opinion Canty had been a lazy, shiftless man, and without a doubt the money he used to buy the house he lived in could only have come from the stagecoach robberies.

Malley then went on to testify as to the tip he received from Roy Smeal, a person well known to him, with regard to Mr. Morgan's possibly dangerous attitude toward the deceased. And so on.

Roy Smeal was called, but was too drunk to testify. Dismissed and admonished by the coroner, who described him as "inebriated and incoherent," the rummy staggered out of the courtroom.

Morgan told his story, with few interruptions from the coroner, and the jury didn't even leave the room to bring in a verdict of justifiable homicide. The coroner thanked

Morgan and expressed sympathy for the terrible ordeal he'd been through.

Malley shook hands with Morgan and gave him some advice before he left. "Listen to me good, son. If you catch any more of those fellas while you're still in town take them well out past the city limits before you kill them. Otherwise good luck and good hunting."

"Thanks for everything, Marshal," Morgan said. He meant it.

Van Wert was waiting at the top of the steps. Morgan walked over to him and said, "The stableman said you wanted to talk to me."

"I've been wanting to talk to you since yesterday." Van Wert's voice was flat, his face deadpan. You've been dodging me, why is that? I could arrest you for obstructing justice, the way you've been dodging me."

Shit! Morgan thought, this bird gets right down to it. "I haven't been dodging you. The robbers left me with nothing, and I had to buy all new gear, even a hat, a shirt, and a watch. Then I had to buy a horse, a saddle. I had to eat and sleep. All that takes time."

Morgan wanted to tell Van Wert to go and fuck himself. The soft answer was better, he decided. At least, for now.

"You slept the first night in a whorehouse," Van Wert said. "Where'd you get the money for that, and the other money you spent? Butterfield said he didn't give you any money."

"I didn't ask him." Van Wert was pushing so hard Morgan wondered how long he could keep his temper.

"If the robbers cleaned us out, where did you find the money? Don't tell me a loan. You're a stranger here and you had nothing to sell, so you say."

Morgan said, "The robbers missed the three gold Mexicans in the lining of my boot. If you don't believe that go talk to the bartenders at the Pearl Saloon. The Pearl Of The West. Three bartenders there, the one that changed the gold piece is short, bald, has a bent nose. Remarked on the coin, said you didn't see them much. Ask him."

All Van Wert did was grunt. "What's this all about?" Morgan said. "A coroner's jury just cleared me of any wrongdoing. You were there; you heard what I said. What is there to add?"

People were still drifting out of the courthouse. Some of them nodded and smiled at Morgan, and one old man came over and asked to shake his hand.

"What this country needs is more young men like you," the old man said. "There's times"—he glanced at Van Wert's badge—"when the law fails us and we got to be our own law. God bless you, and keep up the good work."

The old man went away and Van Wert said, "This is no good, no good trying to talk here. Too public."

Morgan wasn't about to go anywhere private with Van Wert. He thought he could take the bastard, but what good would that do him? Assaulting a federal officer, and so forth. "Crowd'll be gone in a minute, Marshal."

"Over there then." Van Wert pointed to a corner, at the top of the steps, where there were stone benches for people to sit on. A statue of Kit Carson, in granite buckskins, stood in the middle of it. The corner offered some privacy, but not so much that Van Wert could start using his fists and boots.

They sat on a bench and Morgan thought all they needed were pigeons to feed, like in the cities. Malley and the coroner came out last and went down the steps without seeing Morgan and Van Wert. It got quiet after that, and Morgan hoped he wouldn't have to crack Van Wert's head on the base of the statue.

After a pause Van Wert said, "I think you set out to find that man and kill him, and that's what you did, no matter what you said in there. You can deny it all you like, but that's what happened."

"That's not so."

"The marshal knows it and so would the coroner if he wasn't too busy kissing Malley's ass. Anybody who knew Canty, or heard him described, knows he wouldn't stand a chance against you. The man was a weakling. Jumped you with a chair—bullshit! They were breaking down the door and you shot him."

For a man with such a quiet look Van Wert was hotting up pretty fast. Morgan wondered if they'd tangle right there in front of the courthouse.

"With the law there I'd be pretty dumb to kill him without a reason. He jumped me with a chair, I'm telling you." Morgan added, "The jury's verdict backs me up."

"Bullshit! You didn't want the law to take him, so you killed him."

"Why would I do that?" Morgan said.

"Because you have no respect for the law," Van Wert said in a sudden fury. "They'd shamed you—hung you up like a slaughtered hog—and by chance you found Canty, and you killed him."

Morgan thought for a moment. "Suppose—just suppose—I killed him like you say, what would be so wrong about that?"

Van Wert didn't have to think. "Because it's against the law, that's why." He seemed to be making an effort to control his temper. "You got away with it this time, but that better be the end of it. Butterfield says you plan to go after these men."

"That's right."

"You don't have a prayer."

"I caught up with Canty."

"Canty was a fluke. If that drunk hadn't led you to him you'd still be making a nuisance of yourself in saloons."

"Asking questions is how it's done," Morgan said.

"Bullshit! You don't know what you're talking about. Well let me tell you something. I don't want you getting in my way, so I'm telling you here and now stay out of it. Go back to Idaho. Go to work for Butterfield. Do anything you fucking please, just keep away from any place I am."

"That's a deal." Morgan knew Van Wert had a lot more to say.

"I mean it, Morgan."

"I hear what you're saying, Marshal, but it's a free country and I can go where I please, ask any questions I want to. If I find out anything I'll let you know. Some way or another I'll get word to you."

"Didn't I just get through telling you. If you hinder me in my work I'll put you in a federal prison for obstruction of justice, concealing information. You didn't tell the whole truth on the stand. You'd better be speaking it now. What did Canty tell you?"

"Not a thing. I was still prodding him to talk when Malley showed up."

Van Wert said, "It's like nothing I've said is getting through to you, so I'll say it again. Quit as of now or be prepared for trouble. Maybe I can't stop you from making an asshole of yourself playing detective—that depends how much of an interfering asshole you turn out to be—but I will tell you this, so even you'll understand. If by some fluke you find another of these men, and you kill him, I'll put you in a federal prison for twenty years; I swear it. I'll do anything—swear to anything—to fix your wagon. If you know my reputation then you'll know I always finish what I start."

"I hear what you're saying."

"You said that before." Van Wert's temper was going from a simmer to a boil. "But what the fuck does it mean? That you're thinking over what I've said, or you don't give a fuck? Tell me something. Is it what they did to you that's making you so fucking stubborn."

"You could say that."

"All right, they knocked you out and hung you from a gate. Worse things have happened to other men. They didn't cornhole you, did they? You wouldn't want to tell something like that on the witness stand. No witnesses left to tell of it but the robbers. Is that why you have such a hate for them?"

Morgan wanted to hit him in the face. Instead he said calmly, "Nothing like that happened. Now if you're done talking, asking questions, and making threats, I'll be on my way."

Morgan stood up.

"Where are you going?" Van Wert said.

"Away from you. I wouldn't mind if I never saw you again."

"I'm warning you," Van Wert said. "You'll see me soon enough if—"

Morgan walked away before Van Wert could finish making the threat. On his way to the stable he checked to see if Van Wert might be trying to keep a watch on him. Not that he could see. What the hell! Let him follow all he liked, for all the good it would do him. Maybe he could go unnoticed in crowded streets, but away from the town, out in open country, he'd have his work cut out for him.

Morgan drank coffee in a five-stool; he had to stand, it was so crowded. From where he was he could see the street, but no sign of Van Wert, and when he thought about it he decided Van Wert was too full of himself to go sniffing after some wrongheaded dumbbell. More likely he'd follow along at his own pace, making his own inquiries. The thing to do was try to stay ahead of Van Wert for as long as he could. A fine idea, if it worked.

He got another cup of coffee. Silver City was ninety miles away, so this would be his last store-bought coffee for a while. It would be good to get away from the noise and stink of Carson. He wondered how much Van Wert thought he knew. Well he did know a few things—nicknames and descriptions of the four other men—but that wasn't worth shit if Canty had been lying. He didn't think he had. Too bad Malley came breaking down the door before he could get more out of Canty—one last bit of information before he killed him. What the hell had he been saying? He was all set to stick Canty when Malley showed up. Only good thing was that he drew Malley instead of Van Wert.

Butterfield was waiting at the stable when he got there. He hadn't seen him leave the court. It must have been right after the verdict. Butterfield held out his hand and Morgan shook it. Butterfield wasn't the kind of man he took to, but neither were a lot of other men. He had nothing against him.

"I'm relieved you were exonerated," Butterfield said, standing there while Morgan saddled his horse. He was traveling light, taking no more than canned bacon and beans, a coffee pot, a fry pan, and grain for the horse. Butterfield's nervous way of talking was making the horse nervous. He was saying something about Van Wert.

"I talked to him," Morgan said. "He warned me off like I figured."

"But you haven't changed your mind?"

"That's right. But I promised him my fullest cooperation." Morgan wanted to smile.

"I guess he wanted to talk about Canty. Is that what he told you?"

"Some of the talk was about Canty." Morgan wished Butterfield would get the hell out of the way. "I told him there wasn't time to make Canty talk."

Butterfield stared at him. "Is that true? What I mean is, I can understand why you'd want to keep it simple, your account of what happened. But the inquest is over and you've been exonerated and you can tell me in strictest confidence what Canty said. I'm asking not only as a friend—and I consider you a friend despite our short acquaintance—but as a businessman whose business has been severely damaged by these outlaws. What I mean—"

Morgan cut in with, "I got nothing out of Canty but his name. I've got to be going, Mr. Butterfield." He had to suffer another handshake before he mounted up. He couldn't decide if Butterfield was asking questions on his own, or had been primed by Van Wert. Fuck it! Too many handshakes, too many questions.

Butterfield waved after him.

It took him three days to get to Silver City. Starting out there he encountered a fair amount of traffic to and from Carson. Mule-drawn wagons, men on mules leading mules, men on foot leading burros, very few horses, and no women at all. That much traffic tore up the road pretty bad, but it thinned out after about thirty miles.

He kept going long after it was dark, stopping only to water and grain the horse. At about nine o'clock he called it quits for the day. The horse was tired, and so was he. His camp for the night was well off the road, in a hollow out of the wind. He hobbled the new horse and put it on a long tether so it could get at the bunchgrass that grew there. For himself he boiled up coffee and heated the bacon and beans in the fry pan.

Several times during the day he'd checked his back trail—nothing. He didn't expect there would be. An old hand like Van Wert wouldn't let himself get caught flashing binoculars from far off, not unless he was trying to make you edgy. Van Wert knew every trick in the book. Morgan knew his own book of tricks was a lot thinner than Van Wert's. For all that, it had served him well enough in the past.

It got bitter cold, but he slept all right. The next day he rode through two mining camps. A few side roads turned off to mining camps back in the hills. For a good stretch the only human he saw was a ragged, barefoot man digging crazily on the side of a hill.

"I'm digging my own grave," the scarecrow called after him.

The next day, late and dark, he got to Silver City, a place he'd passed through without seeing. It was a lot bigger than Yelverton, Margaret Deakin's dusty patch of a town, something smaller than McHargville. One long main street, with shorter streets branching off it. On a hill above the town a mine was going full blast, the ore crushers thumping steadily. The saloons were open, a few eating places, but the rest of the town was closed up for the night. Morgan stabled his horse and asked the man where he could find Menzies's operation.

The man told him go to the bank, turn left, and walk down a way. Morgan found it and looked it over before he went in. It was much smaller than Butterfield's operation, but then the Butterfield Nevada line had been established in the days of the great John himself, king of the roads. It was newer, better kept, and the main building and the barns and stables and workshops had been painted or whitewashed not long before. Lights were rigged up in one of the barns where a tame Indian was working on the mud-caked wheels of a mud wagon with a wire brush. Except for the Indian, the rest of the operation was shut down for the night.

The times of arrival and departure were chalked on a blackboard beside the door to the office. Inside, the ticket window was open for business, though the next mud wagon wouldn't be leaving until five o'clock the next morning. A clerk wearing a green eyeshade was stamping papers with a rubber stamp. Morgan hesitated before he opened the door. What was he going to say if he found Menzies or was directed to where he could be found? The hell with that. First he'd take a look at the man, then decide if he'd come ninety miles for nothing.

The ticket clerk said Mr. Menzies was gone down the line on business and wouldn't be back until very late, maybe as late as the next morning. It took a silver dollar to get him to explain that Menzies's business was a wagon that tried to get past a rockfall, fell off the road and crashed to the bottom of a five-hundred-foot drop, killing the driver and all the passengers. Morgan promised not to tell Mr. Menzies what the clerk told him. Bad for business, Mr.

Menzies always said, to be giving out bad news.

Well there it was, Morgan thought, another night's wait. He rented a room in the first hotel he came to, paid about half the Carson rate, and that was still too much, with his money running low. Sometime later he was sleeping soundly when somebody knocked on the door. Whoever was out there wasn't Van Wert, not with that hesitant little knock. He looked at his watch and saw he'd been sleeping for four hours or so. The knocking started again.

He took his gun and stood to one side of the door. "Who is it?"

A woman's voice hardly loud enough to be heard. "Open the door and you'll get a pleasant surprise," she said.

"You have the wrong room." Morgan stayed where he was, didn't holster the gun. Either she did have the wrong room, or she was a whore drumming up trade. But nothing about this bare, fairly clean place marked it as a whore hotel. That left only one other explanation: there was a man—or men—with her and she was setting him up to be killed.

"Not interested," he said. "You have the wrong room."

She knocked again. "You'll be missing something very nice if you don't open the door. What are you afraid of?"

Morgan reached over and turned the key, then ducked back. The door opened and a good-looking, dark-haired woman in her early thirties came in carrying an old-fashioned carpetbag. She was slightly on the plump side and gave off a smell of whiskey and cheap perfume. Morgan didn't mind plump women as long as they weren't too plump, and they were pleasant to look at. This one was.

"Hello," she said. "Why are you standing in a corner, and what are you doing with that gun?" His voice was light and would have been pleasant if not for the strain in it. She put the carpetbag on the table beside the bed. "I'm not what you think I am."

Morgan hadn't gotten that far. "Lock the door," he said.

"Why don't you do it?" She opened the bag, reached into it, and put a quart of whiskey and two glasses on the table. "I'm your guest, and you're not being very polite."

"Lock the door," Morgan repeated. If they started blasting at the sound of the key turning, better the lady got it than him.

Frowning prettily, she locked the door and went back and sat on the edge of the bed. Morgan went to the door, unlocked it and looked up and down the hallway. Nobody there. He closed the door and locked it, then looked at the plump, pretty woman.

"What do you think you're doing? If you're not that kind of lady what are you doing in my room?" Morgan thought she might be a little drunk. Good-looking she certainly was.

"I'm not one of those women," she said scornfully. Then she smiled and bounced her backside on the bed. "What I am is a lady kicking up her heels while her husband is visiting his sweetheart in San Francisco. He visited her all the time when we lived there. But then his company sent him here—he's a mining engineer—and now he can visit her only twice a year. . . ."

Something wasn't right about her, but he couldn't figure out what it was. No doubt this husband of hers was doing what she said—she was so positive about it—and this was her way of paying him back. He passed on the idea that she was tied in with Van Wert or the stage robbers. It had to be something else.

"You do this twice a year?" he said.

"Oh no," she said. "This is my first time. We've been married for fourteen years, since I was nineteen, but he grew tired of me after the first year. There were other sweethearts before the sweetheart he has now. It's taken me thirteen years to get up the nerve to do this. Don't tell me you don't find me appealing."

"Nothing like that." Morgan sat down beside her. "You took me by surprise, that's all."

"And I have more in store for you," she said.

Chapter Seven

"I don't like surprises," Morgan said. "Could you give me some idea what this surprise might be?"

"Why don't you wait and see? Please fix me a drink while you're waiting. And don't tell me to do it myself, like you did with locking the door."

Morgan gave her the drink and she said, "Why don't you fix one for yourself. I don't like to drink alone. Drinking alone is is how people become drunkards."

Morgan still couldn't figure her. It was like she was putting on an act that wasn't natural to her. Odd thing was he believed her when she said this was her first time looking for cock outside the marriage bed. So maybe her act was no act at all, just the carry-on of an unhappy, lonely woman who was nerving herself up to take the first plunge into adultery.

"I see you looking at me," she said. "Looking and thinking."

"How can I not look and think," Morgan said.

"Am I nice to look at?"

"Very nice." And she was. With her round face, blue eyes, and rosebud mouth, she reminded him of a china doll. A little tired, or a lot tired, no color in her cheeks, but that could be the whiskey and the wandering husband whose cock-happy visits to Frisco made her drink it.

She lay back on the bed with her skirt hiked up and her legs open. Morgan saw that she wasn't wearing drawers and wondered if she wanted to be fucked with her clothes on. He'd run into women like that. With some it was just a peculiarity; others had to get home to fix supper for Rufus and the kids.

"You sure you want to go through with this?" Morgan had already decided that he did. Why look a gift horse in the mouth? He hoped it wouldn't turn out like the story of the starving man who was killed by a gold bar falling from the top story of the mint.

"Need you ask such a question?" She bounced her backside and the bedsprings twanged. "But I would like another drink before we commence."

Commence. There's a word for you, Morgan thought. Maybe she was a schoolteacher when she wasn't doing this. *Let us commence our lesson, children.*

"But I refuse to drink another drop unless you join me," she said. "Loosen up, for heaven's sake—get into the spirit of things."

Morgan's cock was more in the spirit than his head was. He still had suspicious of her—something wasn't right here—but he knew his cock was going to win by a nose. Fuck it! He didn't know where Van Wert was. Probably out there under the starry sky, lecturing the prairie dogs on law and order. A joke, son. The sour joke faded when he thought of Margaret Deakin, the friendly scattershot talk, the sandwiches. He had to make it right for her—this here was bullshit.

Morgan belted back the drink he didn't want and got on to the bed beside her. She came right into his arms, and he started to take off her clothes. She fought him a little in the beginning, as if she thought leaving her drawers at home was enough, but then she loosened up, as she'd told him to do, and after that she was all eager for him to strip her bare. And when he had her in the altogether and was ready to commence she hiccuped and said, the whiskey talking: "It seems I'm a Rubens woman. At thirty-three I'm turning into a Rubens woman, my husband says. Now you've got my clothes off how'd you like me?"

Morgan knew a Joe Ruben, a job printer in Boise. No other Rubens he could think of.

"Rubens was a Dutch artist who painted very ample women," she said. "My husband likes them slender, like willow trees. I was like a willow tree before I married him. Too much potatoes and fatty bacon. Now I'm ample."

"You're not that ample," Morgan said gallantly. And she wasn't. Five more years of spuds and fatback would make her more than ample. A mining engineer ought to be able to put better food on the table. Maybe he was a gambler, or was sending half what he made to the sweetheart in Frisco. He sure as hell wasn't spending money on his wife. The dress he'd just taken off her wasn't patched, but it had seen better days. Enough of that. Time to get to it.

At first there was some slight resistance, but it disappeared after he got all the way in. Her juices began to flow and his cock felt like it was shafting in warm, sweet honey. She was a real handful, just what the doctor ordered for cold winter nights, and her cushioned ass felt nice in his big hands. As soon as he got going right so did she, and she gave out little breathy whispers that meant nothing to him. He thought he caught the name "Martin," and that could've been the husband's name or the name of somebody she'd known long ago. It could've been the name of a brother or some handsome actor she'd seen in a traveling show.

Now she was enjoying it as much as he was, no more payback to the husband. Not that a revenge fuck didn't have its good points—some women were like wildcats—but it could be punishing if they had long fingernails. Nothing like that here: she wanted it for its own sake. She locked her legs around the small of his back, and he fucked her steadily, sucking one nipple, then the other, and her crotch ground into his as excitement took hold of her and her body began to writhe. The bed creaked good and loud as his shafting picked up speed, and she bucked so hard it took some effort to hold her down, and it looked like she was trying to get more cock into her than there were inches. Morgan was long and thick and strong, but she wanted more. The way she gasped told him that, and he did his best to oblige. Everything he did to her made her gasp. Her ass spasmed in his hands and her own sweat-slick hands wandered up his body and buried themselves in his hair. There was some pain as her grip on his hair increased, but that just made him pump faster. Suddenly, with a loud gasp and an upward lurch that nearly threw him off the bed, she came so violently that it felt like she was having a fit. Her eyes rolled back into her head, and he saw a trickle of blood where her teeth bit her lower lip. And it didn't stop with that. Morgan thrust into her and came with a violence that matched hers, and even when he was drained and moving just to be moving she kept on coming and coming. "Don't stop," she whispered. "Don't take it out. Leave it in and I'll make you hard again. Let me move now. Let me make it hard."

The words came out in gasps, and she kept trembling even when her string of comes had finally ebbed. It was like the salvo of orgasms had made her cunt so sensitive that it convulsed or relaxed in response to the slightest movement of his cock. And she moved her cunt and her ass and her hands, her whole body, as she said she would. Morgan was content to lie on top of her soft, white body and let her do the work. It was pure pleasure, he thought, to let her do the work, and he hoped the wandering husband was having as good a time as he was.

The only time she stopped was when she got herself a big, quick drink and insisted that he have one too. With the table and the bottle so close, she was able to pour the drinks with his cock still in her. The gulped-down drink would hit her hard in a minute, Morgan knew. That was all right. He didn't want his own drink, but he drank it. It took more than two drinks to give him a soft cock. Before she settled back she said, "Rubens wasn't a Dutch artist. He was Flemish. I must remember to get that right. My—"

That was the end of that, and Morgan was glad of it. One ample woman at a time was enough for him. Lord but she was working hard to get him ready again. Nothing wrong with that—surely and certainly not—though he couldn't quite see why she was in such a hurry. Well, yes, he could when he thought about it. If she hadn't enjoyed cock for a long time—it looked like she hadn't—she'd be like the bad-off man in the desert who finally gets to water or is given some. Wanting more and more even if it makes him sick. Too much cock wouldn't make her sick, but the whiskey might. It would be a bitch of a thing to have happen.

But it looked like there was no danger of a messy bed. The sheets were tangled, and the air was thick with come and sweat, but that was a good smell. Her hand was playing with his balls and his cock began to stiffen. It'd been no time since he'd shot a good measure into her, but there was the evidence. His cock was ready for another offensive, so to speak, and his balls were moving into position to back it up. "See how big and hard I made it," she whispered as her crotch began to bump in time with his thrusts. "I'm going to wear you out with—"

What she left unsaid didn't matter, and it did look like she meant to wear him out. Such energy this woman had! If such a thing could be said, she was fucking him harder than he was fucking her. It went on like that, with no let up, and she gave as good as she got, which was considerable, and then some. No stopping for a drink this time, and it looked like Martin, or whoever he was, was forgotten. The only whispering she did was about how big and long his cock was, how much she wanted it and needed it, and do it harder, do it harder.

Doing it as hard as he could, Morgan didn't smile though her eyes were closed. All that whispering was meant to keep him up to the mark. No need for it, not a bit, he was going like a pile driver. It was funny the way she talked, like she was taking pains to talk proper, even here in this rumpled bed. And it wasn't just the words but the way she said them. Very clear and fancy like, as if she'd practiced talking in front of a mirror. Could be. Why not?

She came again and so did he. His come was good, but she came like she was jumping out of her skin, leaping and plunging until the bed threatened to fall apart. After she calmed down a bit he kissed her and tried to roll off so he could rest. Not a long rest, just a rest. But she wanted none of that, and the whispering started again. Didn't he want to go on? Was he tired of her in such a short time? Don't do a thing—just lie there—and I'll make it hard again.

Morgan rolled off, but she wouldn't let him rest. She stroked his cock and fondled his balls, all the time whispering how she wanted him to get hard so he could "do it" again. She didn't say cock or fuck. What she was doing was all right with Morgan. All he had to do was lie there and stroke her hair after she left off stroking his cock and began to suck it.

He would have been happy to come that way, but she wanted him in her. Three times in a row, with no rest between them, was pushing it, even for him. But he rallied, and once again he was shafting her with as much energy as he could muster while she fucked as furiously as before, urging him on, begging him not to let up. Finally he came and there was the feeble hope that now, at long last, she'd let him rest for a while. Her own come was fierce and long lasting. After it dwindled down to heavy breathing and an occasional shudder, she made no protest when he rolled off her and lay on his back.

"I've got to rest a bit," he said before she could start again with his cock. To have a good-looking woman fooling with your cock was no rest at all. Too bad if she thought he was letting her down, but there it was. He needed a rest, no two ways about it. Later he'd fuck her to a fare-thee-well, but for now. . . .

"You were wonderful," she said. Mercy, lady! Morgan thought. Then with a yawn she added, "I think we both need a rest. A little sleep will work wonders." Morgan started to doze off even as she said it.

He opened his eyes when he felt her reaching over toward the table. The bottle and glasses were there, so was the carpetbag. Maybe she needed another drink to help her drop off. But there was no clink of bottle and glass, just a faint rummaging sound from the carpetbag. A two-shot derringer was pointing at his face when he turned his head. His hand closed over her hand and the gun before she could cock it. He tore the gun from her hand and knocked her cold before she could scream. It was a short blow, and he was able to grab her before she went off the bed. He climbed over her with the gun in his hand. Before he looked in the carpetbag he unloaded the derringer and put it under the bed. He didn't know what he expected to find in the bag. Anything he found out about her would be more than he knew. The philandering-husband story was bullshit.

In the bag, among other things, he found a letter addressed to Mrs. Buford De Forest, Silver City, Nevada. It had been mailed from Topeka, Kansas, a week before. He made sure she was still unconscious before he read it.

* * *

Dear Babs,

It pains me to do so, but I must refuse your request for a loan of fifty dollars, for, as we both know, such a loan would never be repaid, no matter how many promises my unfortunate brother makes to the contrary. As of now, he is indebted to me in the sum of one hundred and ninety dollars, and no more will be forthcoming. In the past, because of brotherly concern, I'd helped him to obtain positions with a number of respectable firms, and always he has let me down, absconding from his job at the Topeka Grain Company with the petty cash, not a great sum, to be sure, but for which I accepted responsibility and felt honor bound to "make good." Martin could have been a respected attorney by now, if he had applied himself to his studies. Instead, he has chosen to live the life of a wandering gambler, an occupation for which he is totally unfitted. Gambling has been and will continue to be the cause of his ruination, and of yours, unless he conquers this terrible addiction, and this, I am afraid is too much to hope for. Changing his name to "Buford De Forest" is surely a sign of how completely he has lost himself in the land of dreams. If poor misguided Martin wants so desperately to establish himself among the landed gentry, he must do better than to change his name and talk extravagantly of his "Southern ancestors."

I must close now.

Sincerely yours,

John Knox Heckwelder

There it was, Morgan thought. Just like that. Gent was Martin Heckwelder, known to Silver City and other places as Buford De Forest. He looked at the woman on the bed. If she hadn't come to kill him there was nothing to connect Gent with Silver City. He'd come looking for Menzies and found Gent instead. Well he hadn't found him yet, but he would. The brother was right. Buford De Forest sounded like a tinhorn gambler, the kind of julep sippin' Ole Massa name a tinhorn would pick. He'd met them in his travels, the tinhorns with the wide hats and frock coats, the Dixie accents, the string ties. A few were real Southern gents down on their luck. Most were fakers like Heckwelder, and that was understandable enough. What didn't fit was how a shithole like Heckwelder got mixed up in the stage robbing business, and who in hell would pick him to be part of a gang? By the same token, who would recruit somebody like Tobe Canty? But the big question was how did Heckwelder get word so fast? It had to be the telegraph, and if so, who sent the message? And from where?

He slapped her awake and she lay there wanting to kill him. It was in her eyes. He didn't know how he felt about her. In a way he couldn't fault her for trying, and whatever she was, she was better than Heckwelder deserved.

"Hello, Babs," he said, showing her the letter. "No lying now or you'll be sorry for it. Where's your husband?"

She felt her jaw. It was beginning to swell. "I'm going to scream. I'm going to bring the clerk and the marshal up here. I'm going to say you forced me up here and raped me at gunpoint."

Morgan was glad he was dressed. If she did scream it was better they didn't find him bare assed. They might lynch him before the marshal got a chance to lock him up. And if he was given time to explain, who would believe him?

"You got me past the desk because the clerk was sleeping," she said. "Claude is old and likes to sleep. Everybody knows that." There was defiance as well as hate in her eyes.

Pretty quick thinking, Morgan thought. "Go ahead and scream. Do it. I'm the one who should be screaming for help. You near broke my back."

She called him a filthy degenerate.

"Where's your husband?" he said again.

"Gone," she said, raising up on one elbow. "Gone where you'll never find him. He's in California by now, and you'll never find him. He's been gone for days."

"Then how did he get onto me? By telegraph?"

"That's for you to find out."

"I could beat it out of you."

"Not here. Try it, and I'll scream my head off."

Morgan knew she had him there. If he couldn't beat the truth out of her, threats were useless. But even if he could slap her around, he wasn't going to do it. Instead he told her what her husband and his pals had done to Margaret Deakin, leaving out no details of the rape, the savaged breasts, the broken teeth, the torn-out hair. He finished with, "She was on her way to be married, but couldn't face her man the way she was. She cut her throat. I buried her."

It took Mrs. Heckwelder a while to answer. "You're lying. My husband would never be a part of that. How could he? He wasn't there. He was with me in the restaurant all that day you say it happened. I'll swear to it."

"You run a restaurant?" It figured that Heckwelder had to have some money coming in to make up for his gambling losses.

"It's an honest living. My husband was with me all the time, from early morning till late at night. After I closed up he helped me fix the next day's stew."

"Anybody see him there?"

"I don't know. Probably. Most of the day he was doing carpenter work out back."

Lord how she could lie, Morgan thought. The husband sounded like he couldn't drive a nail into a soft pine board. Didn't matter what she said, he wasn't going to get anything out of her unless she tripped herself up, or he could stir her conscience with Margaret Deakin's pointless death.

He tried the last. "Margaret Deakin was a nice, decent young woman. But no woman—good or bad—deserves what they did to her. I mean to catch them and put them in jail. Let the law deal with them."

"You're lying!" she shouted in sudden anger. Morgan got set for footsteps on the stairs, banging on the door. Nothing happened. She lowered her voice, but it remained fierce. "You already killed one man. I heard you killed one man. It was in the paper."

Maybe it was, Morgan thought. It had taken him three days to get to Silver City. It could have been in the paper. "I had to kill him," he said. "Self-defense. A coroner's jury cleared me. That should have been in the paper."

It wasn't working. Nothing he said was working. "I don't care what you say. I don't believe you. My husband is gone, and I don't know where. Beat me all you like. I won't tell you so you can kill him."

"Get out," Morgan said.

But she wanted to have her say. "Don't think I'll lead you to him. I'll stay right here until I hear from him. Maybe he's not the big, strong man you think you are. But you'd better be careful—he can ride, and he can shoot."

Ride and shoot. Could be he'd taken the time to learn how to do both, part of the Buford De Forest idea he had of himself. "He's so brave he sent you."

"He's no murderer and no coward."

No, he just rides with killers, Morgan thought. He was tired of her talk, and his own. "Get out."

"I'll get out all right!" Her heels landed hard and the floor shook. He watched as she pulled on her clothes, tugging angrily at the straps and buttons. She tossed the bottle and glasses into the bag and something broke. "Where's my gun? Damn you! I can get another gun."

She went out without closing the door. The last thing she said was, "I wish I'd killed you."

Morgan closed the door and waited for morning.

Chapter Eight

First thing he headed for the stable where his horse was. Maybe they could tell him if Heckwelder owned a horse, not too likely, or rented one for his stage robbing forays. If they didn't know, he would have to try the other liveries. He didn't see any eating place called Buford's Eats. If the restaurant was real it could be on some side street, but it wouldn't be called that. Elegant Southern gentlemen like Buford wouldn't want his name associated with a liver and onions emporium. No sign of Mrs. Heckwelder, with or without a gun.

A few minutes before, coming down from his room, he saw the elderly night clerk sleeping soundly, a pillow behind his head, his feet on a box. It was just after five-thirty, and the day man hadn't come on yet. The town was quiet except for the steady thumping of the ore crushers up above it. A few stores were opening up, getting ready for the day's business. The Western Union office stayed open all night; he had business there later.

A deputy marshal propping up the front of the jail looked after him. He wasn't a miner, didn't have a familiar face. In the stable the same man Morgan saw the night before was rubbing down a horse, making the hissing sound grooms make. Morgan had tipped him before he left the horse, always a good idea, and got a friendly "Morning" when he went in.

"Sure I know Buford," the man said, cheerful, though sober. "Owing you money, is he? Buford owes ever'body money, them as is foolish enough to loan it. Hell no! Buford don't own no horse. Owned a right good horse back a way. Sold it, later on bought another good one, sold that too. Now he rents a horse when he needs it. I make him pay in advance. Say this for him, always has money to rent good horseflesh."

"Did he rent a horse the last day or two?" Morgan was turning a fifty cent piece between his fingers.

"Rented one, day before yesterday, late evening," the man said. "Sure I'm sure. Marked it down in my book, you want to see it. Afraid I can't help you with the direction he took. Only two ways you can go from here, on to McHarville or back to Carson. Course there's roads going into the back country. I doubt if Buford was headed in there. They'd eat him alive, those wild settlements."

Morgan gave him the fifty cents. "You could ask his wife. She has a beanery on Washoe Street," the man called after him.

Morgan started back for the telegraph office. The bastard had a day and a half start on him, and wasn't riding a nag; that would give him an extra edge. The hell of it was he could be heading any of three ways. Morgan scrubbed the back country for now. Maybe he wouldn't head for Carson because of Van Wert. But why not? Even if he met Van Wert on the road, Van Wert wouldn't know him from his grandmother. Toss a coin, Morgan thought. Maybe the telegraph clerk could tell him something.

That didn't seem too likely when he got a close-up look at the elderly man writing busily in a book on the counter. Morgan didn't like his look of lifelong rectitude, hymns sung, church suppers attended. No early morning dozing for this geezer, no coffee steaming beside him, no tobacco smoke. He had a long face, long white hair, righteous blue eyes.

"Yes, sir," he said, reaching for a message form.

No easy way to slide into it with this old man, so Morgan asked straight out. "Any telegrams come for Mr. or Mrs. Buford De Forest the last day or two? Something like that." Later Morgan couldn't recall what he'd said. However he said it, it didn't go down like gravy.

"I'm a—" Morgan said.

"That's right," the old man said. "What are you? Who are you?"

Morgan gave his right name. The old man glared at the silver dollar he put on the counter, told him if he didn't want to send a telegram to put the money back in his pocket and begone.

Morgan put the tainted coin in his pocket. "I'm not supposed to tell you this"—he lowered his voice—"but I'm working with U.S. Marshal Jake Van Wert. Investigating the stage robberies this stretch of road. Mr. Van Wert wants to keep it hush-hush for now. I guess you heard of Jake Van Wert all right."

Van Wert's celebrity, if the old man knew of it, didn't impress him. "Anybody can say anything. You better show me a badge, mister."

Another ditch to get over. "I don't carry a badge. See, I'm not a regular lawman, just gathering information for the marshal. I'm—"

"You're no kind of a lawman, that's what you are."

"You better tell me, old man."

The old man's eyes flashed fire. "Old I may be, you reprobate! Not so old I can't deal with the likes of you. Marshal Van Wert shows up here he's going to hear plenty about you. How do I know you ain't a stage robber yourself? You got a mean look to you—"

Morgan got out of there before the geezer reached for a gun. Telegraph offices took in money. There could be a gun under the counter. He hoped the old man wouldn't go running to the marshal. The marshal might try to hold him for Van Wert. Not try. With deputies to back him he could do it. Maybe he should head out right now. He'd played it wrong, but maybe there was no right way. It was just his luck to draw a tough, honest old man who couldn't be bribed or intimidated. Fuck it! He'd come to talk to Menzies, and that's what he'd do. Maybe he could get a few answers before the law put him in irons.

A different ticket clerk told him Mr. Menzies might not want to see him so early. Which meant Menzies could be asleep in his office. Was it urgent business? Morgan said urgent enough. The clerk got Morgan's name and went down a hallway to check. At first there was shouting, then that stopped, and a loud voice said, "Send him in."

Menzies was big and bulky but didn't fill the doorway. The man Canty called Bear would have filled it, would have had to stoop his head to get through it. Canty said Bear's hair was thick and wild, streaked with gray. Menzies hair was soft and light colored, thinning on top, and plastered down with something.

"What can I do for you, lad?" Menzies said, tired looking but lively, holding out a thick, rough hand. "I'm Niven Menzies, at your service, sir." They shook hands, and he gestured Morgan toward a chair before he sat behind his desk. "Mr. Morgan, is it?"

Morgan said it was, knowing damn well Menzies didn't have to have his memory jogged. Selecting what he wanted to say—for now—he told Menzies about the robbery, what had happened to Margaret Deakin.

"Ah, yes," Menzies said. "Some of that was in the paper, some more was added. Surely you weren't carrying the ten thousand the paper says you lost?"

"More like ninety." Menzies sounded something like Bear, but there was a lilt to his voice that Bear's didn't have, no growl at all. If Canty's description wasn't bullshit, Menzies wasn't Bear.

Morgan knew Menzies was sizing him up, doing it openly, and when he spoke again his voice wasn't so friendly. "Now, sir, allowing for what you went through—that poor woman—what is it that brings you here? Is it because one of the men sounded like a Scotchman, you think? Well you know, I don't keep track of every Scotchman in Nevada." The voice took on a real edge. "Or is it because you think I had something to do with it. I'm big and I'm Scotch, is that it? Be a man, for Christ's sake, and say what you came to say."

"I was wrong," Morgan said. "You were described to me. It doesn't fit. I apologize. I'm still hoping you can help me."

Menzies rubbed his face. Morgan could see he was dog tired. "Who did the describing? Butterfield? It would be just like him to set you on me. I know it wasn't Malley. That amiable old grafter lives in his own fat little world and has no interest outside it. Did Butterfield tell you I served eight years in Sing-Sing?"

"I didn't say Butterfield said—"

Menzies jolted forward in his swivel chair. "Talk straight or get the fuck out of here. What did Butterfield say?"

What the hell, Morgan thought. He didn't owe Butterfield a thing. Well maybe the favor with the horse, but that didn't put him in debt for life. Each of the men who killed Margaret Deakin owed a life. Still, he didn't want to do Butterfield any harm.

"Now hear me out," he said. "Butterfield didn't accuse you of anything—"

"Like hell he didn't."

"Will you let me talk. I asked Butterfield who might want to ruin his business and buy it cheap."

"And right off he said me."

"Not like that. I had to prod him a bit."

"The hell you did."

"He said you'd been looking into the state of his business, with a mind to buy. He gave out it wasn't for sale. Is that right?"

Menzies was cagey for all his bluff manner. "Right enough. A lawyer did it for me. The lawyer said other interested parties were doing the same thing, only natural."

"Then you're not behind these robberies? You'd asked me to talk straight."

Menzies laugh was big, like the rest of him. "By God, you've got a lot of nerve for your size." Morgan was over six feet. "Let me answer a question with a question. Look around you, what do you see? A good, sound business, is what. You want to walk to the bank with me so the manager can tell you how good I'm doing? Does that answer your question?"

Morgan shook his head. "You're doing good; you might want to do better."

"Ah yes, the greedy businessman, can't get enough. Now listen. I'm taking the time to listen to you when I could be getting some much-needed sleep. I'm explaining myself to you, but I don't have to. All right. They call me Sing-Sing behind my back. I'll never live that down, not even if I get to be the richest man in the state, and a senator to boot. What I don't want is to do a thing that will land me back behind the walls. If they had a real sidewalk here I wouldn't spit on it. If I found a dollar I'd turn it in to the marshal and make him give me a receipt. You don't know what it's like behind the walls."

Looking at Menzies, Morgan had some idea of what it must have been like. A big man like that locked up in a cramped cell with two or three other men. The queers would bother anybody. Would even bother a big man that could swat them like a fly. Bother him quicker because of that. Being locked up would be the worst part of it.

"I believe you," Morgan said.

"I could be lying."

"Not about breaking the law. And not breaking it. But you wanted Butterfield's line more than you said."

"Smart as a whip, that's you. All right, I had a strong mind to buy it, still do. But what about yourself? You come in here with your story of killing a man in self-defense, Boss and Bear and Little Bear and Gent. What else haven't you told me?"

Morgan told him about Mrs. Heckwelder.

Menzies shook his head in wonder. "There's a woman for you! Fucks you cross-eyed then tries to put the Big Kibosh on you. Wouldn't be a bad way to die, come to think of it. I must say I've noticed her more than him. Yes, sure I have. A real armful, that lady. A pity she puts on such a glum face. Understandable from what I know, and what you tell me. Will give you a nod in the street, no more than that."

"The husband—"

"Can't tell you much about him. Well you have to look at him, the way he dresses, Doc Holiday's hand-me-downs. Always well turned out though, no doubt the good lady's doing. I'll bet she even waxes his mustache. I can't say how good he does at the tables. Not so good, I would think. You say the wife runs a restaurant? Can't say I know it. I don't eat in restaurants. My Chinaman does fine by me."

"It's likely a small place," Morgan said.

Menzies smacked his lips. "I wouldn't mind sampling some of her savories. I envy you."

"Then you can't tell me much about Heckwelder?"

"Afraid not." Menzies was back down to earth. "But I've been thinking, about the one you call Bear. You meet so many people in my business. This goes back before the robberies, I'm pretty sure about that. A big Calgary Scotchman—huge man—came looking for a job in the barns. Took no more than a few minutes to decide

I couldn't use him. Had a brutal look about him—I don't mean his size—I knew he'd be mean to the animals. There may be nothing in this."

"You get his name?"

"Hamish Fife is the name he gave me, could be his real one. No business of mine what it was. I didn't want him. Later on—I don't know exactly when—I was surprised to hear he'd bought a decent-sized place about thirty or forty miles down the road, somewhere near Beal's Creek, that's just a few houses, a drinking place, a general store."

Menzies rubbed his face. "I guess McAllister must have mentioned it to me. McAllister is active in the Knights of St. Andrew. The Scotch Knights of Columbus. Does that help you?"

"You don't know if he has a son?"

"Little Bear? That I can't say. All I know is what I told you. Could have a wife and ten sons for all I know. Looked like a drunkard that can hold it. I hate drunkards. Drunken fight got me Sing-Sing."

The ticket clerk came in without knocking and told Menzies he was needed in the repair shop. A jacked-up wagon had fallen on a man, injuring him bad. The clerk ran out saying something about the doctor. Menzies came out from behind the desk.

"You can wait if you like," he said to Morgan.

"No, I'd better be going. Thanks."

Menzies looked at him. "That man Canty, it wasn't self-defense, was it?"

Morgan gave him a sour smile. "What do you think?"

"Good man." Menzies clapped him on the arm and went out ahead of him.

Morgan went back to the livery stable, keeping an eye out for the marshal. By now another deputy was propping up the jail. More people were in the street now, and Morgan didn't get a second look. So maybe the old telegraph clerk was saving his story for Van Wert. Didn't want to waste it on these local no-accounts with badges.

Morgan passed another deputy and the man didn't even turn his head.

So it was safe to eat breakfast and see if Babs was open for business. Odd thing was he felt no real ill will toward the woman. She did what she did. Anyway, Morgan always found it hard to carry a grudge for a woman, no matter how dangerous, and it was even harder when she was good-looking. Menzies was right to be jealous. Mrs. Heckwelder's savories were tasty.

Good Food was the name of the place—a touch of class there—not Eats, and it was open. Morgan rode past and saw her rubbing at the steamed-up window to get a better look at him. He didn't wave at her for fear she'd come after him with a cleaver. Joke time was over. He couldn't think of any jokes he wanted to make about Hamish Fife.

After he cleared the in-coming traffic, mostly wagons, he made good time. He pushed the gelding hard because this time he had a name, a place where this Hamish Fife could be found. Menzies said there might be nothing in it. Morgan didn't think so. Things were beginning to fit, and this time if he worked it right, there would be no law butting in. Sudden anger took hold of him as he thought of the next man he had to kill. That was no good. He'd bollix it up if he went in like that. He had to let up on the horse.

Good advice. Why didn't he take it? Ten miles down the road, resting the horse, letting it drink, he was still twanging with impatience. Wanting to get on with it, to find Hamish Fife, to make him talk, to kill him and move on—to where? That was the thing that stuck in his craw. What if Hamish Fife turned out to be a dead end? Heckwelder had a long start, and it would be a lot longer by the time he finished with Fife. But there was no help for that. Fife was a bird in the hand—probably was—and Heckwelder was—where?

The worst of it was, the tinhorn could be anywhere. Halfway to Carson. Riding hard for McHargville. Hiding in the hills just outside Silver City. He was like the man in the story who kept hitting himself over the head and all the time complaining of how much it hurt. Then why was he doing it? Because he was impatient, wanted to get it over with, et cetera. But he had to stop the head beating, had to steady down, to learn to be patient. He felt weary when he thought of how patient he'd have to be if Hamish Fife came up dry. All he could do—goddamit!—was to keep on going. No other way to do it. Got to be patient, yes, sir. Patience my ass!

By late afternoon, best as he could figure, he had come more than twenty miles, with ten miles to go before he reached Beal's Creek. Menzies said Fife's place was some miles beyond there, how many he wasn't sure. He didn't want to show himself in the settlement, but he had to ask where Fife's place was. No other easy way to find it. Later, after Fife was dead, when the law started asking questions, somebody—maybe a lot of people—would remember his face, how he was dressed, the rest of it. The county sheriff might follow it up, or he might not. Nevada, not as wild as it used to be, was still wild enough, and the law was loose. However it went, he had come too far to have second thoughts.

The light was just about gone when he got close to the settlement. He got off the road and glassed it from a distance, shading the binoculars with his hat. There was no creek that he could see, and only a straggle of houses and shacks. He must have slept through it on the way to Carson. It wasn't a change station and no passengers got on. Supper smoke spiraled up from chimneys, drifted on the wind. It was quiet.

Six horses were hitched in front of the saloon, two of them farm animals. The general store next to it was closed. Both places had the same name over the door: Tom Early. A farmer-looking man came out of the saloon, got on a workhorse, and walked it out of town. Still too many men in there, Morgan thought. Could be other men from the town who didn't need a horse to get there, maybe ten or twelve men in all.

Asking where Fife lived would draw attention no matter how he did it. That Cousin Jethro act wouldn't work here, too foolish. All he could do was ask where Hamish Fife had his place and let it go at that. He didn't have to explain, but he'd have to buy a beer or two before he asked. They'd be suspicious—damn right they'd be suspicious—might look him up and down before they told him where Fife was. Fife worked a place near here, so he wasn't a stranger. Morgan was.

In the morning, he thought, as soon as the saloon opened. Beals Creek wasn't an all-night town. At that hour there would be nobody there but the proprietor, maybe one or two early-bird drunks downing their first drink of the day. Of course, even a drunk could rush off to warn Fife that there was a stranger snooping around. That had happened with Canty, but there was a difference. Here he'd just ask after Fife, wouldn't start describing him, and so on. If one of them thought he had to warn Fife—for friendship or money—Morgan figured to head him off before he got there. He hoped that wouldn't happen. After all, he could hardly kill the man, just rope and gag him, and let him loose on the way back. A man left like that could die in no time. It was enough to kill the men he was after, and not go killing some fool.

He grained and watered the horse and tied it to a well-rooted thornbush. Strong black coffee was what he wanted most, but he went without it. Even a small fire might be seen. He ate supper out of a can and drank water from his canteen. It got cold and he wrapped up good before he went to sleep.

Chapter Nine

Van Wert got off his horse and went into the saloon. Morgan had been watching him since he saw him coming along the road from Silver City, moving at a fast clip. It was seven o'clock in the morning, already warming up, and the saloon had been open for no more than five minutes.

Morgan was set to head in when he heard the rider approaching. He was behind a ridge a long way back from the road, but he didn't need the binoculars to recognize Van Wert. Now he was in there asking his questions, and describing Morgan, as no doubt he'd done in Silver City and the smaller towns along the road.

A good thing he hadn't headed in a few minutes earlier. It could have come to gunplay if Van Wert had tried to stop him. So close to Fife he couldn't let that happen, and he sure as hell wasn't going to submit to arrest, if Van Wert had it in mind. He didn't want to tangle with Van Wert, not if it meant one of them dead when it was over, yet he got the feeling that such a thing was entirely possible.

It seemed like Van Wert was in there a long time. But he saw that wasn't so when he looked at his watch. Van Wert came out, swung himself into the saddle, and rode out fast. The saloon keeper came out and looked after him, scratching his beard, then went back inside.

Morgan gave it a few minutes. Still nobody there but the saloon keeper when he walked in. Doing something with bottles behind the bar, the man tried not to look surprised when he looked up. Not much of his face could be seen because of the beard, but it was in his eyes.

"Mornin'," he said, holding up a beer mug. "Beer?"

Morgan nodded. "A beer would be good." He put money on the bar. The saloon was like the town, dusty and broken down. The bar was like a regular bar except not too well made and not too many bottles stood on the shelf behind it. No tables and chairs.

The beer tasted good. The man gave him a sly look and said, "You just missed a man lookin' for you. U.S. Marshal Van Wert he said he was. I guess he was, showed me his badge."

"Fine man, Jake," Morgan said, drinking the beer. "Too bad I missed him."

The man took Morgan's empty mug. "You can catch up to him if you hurry." He put the fresh beer in front of Morgan.

"No hurry. Jake'll probably wait for me along the way."

"If he don't turn about and come back, that is." The man threw the money in a bowl under the counter. "Well, I know you must be friends 'cause he didn't say one bad thing about you. It was like he wanted to talk to you real bad."

"That's Jake for you," Morgan said, "always in a hurry. Then he asked about Hamish Fife.

That got another sly look, real foxy this time. "Funny, the marshal didn't ask for him at all."

Morgan put two silver dollars on the counter. Time was wasting, gabby drunks could be on their way. "Two's the limit," he said. "You know where Fife is?"

The two dollars clattered into the bowl. "Here's how you get there, no great distance. But I will ask you keep it under your hat who sent you. Hamish is not a nice fella when he has too much whiskey in him, which I am sorry to say is most of the time. Last time he was here he thought to demolish the place with his bare hands, and it took five of us and a bung starter to get rid of him. Now he sends his son for his whiskey. A fine pair, the two of them."

Morgan thanked the man and left. Out of town about two miles, on the turnoff road the man had said. Morgan got up behind a hill and watched for anyone coming from town. If they came they'd be riding hard. The saloon keeper didn't have to come himself, he could send somebody. But that wasn't likely, the way he told the story on Fife. Morgan gave it ten minutes and then moved on.

It was empty and quiet up here, not a wagon or rider in sight. As he moved into the hills it was hard to think much of anything could be raised, crops or animals, in this bleak, sun-scorched country. Yet there it was. It was being tried. Fife was trying it. Water was the key to it. You could make the poorest land fertile if you had water.

Fife's place was a good ten miles back from the main road, the saloon keeper had said. Then you turned off the side road onto a worse road and Fife's place was a mile or so in from there. The saloon keeper doubted there would be a sign, but that didn't matter. Fife's road, more of a track, was all there was along there and you couldn't miss it.

No use trying to figure it before he saw how it was. At least he only had two of them to deal with. Like Menzies said, Fife could have ten sons, all as bad as himself. Fife and just one son would be bad enough. He couldn't get a picture of the son. Apart from Hamish Fife himself there was only one other big man among the robbers, so that had to be him.

He walked his horse for the last few miles. Coming in fast would kick up dust sure to be spotted by a lookout in a high place. High places were few in these parched hills, bare except for sage and thorn, but there were some. No wind blew, not even a dusty breeze, and the sun was merciless.

He found the road to Fife's place and rode past it, walking the horse for another half mile before he started across country. After a while he had to get down and lead the horse. At times, when he had to climb over a hill, he could see the road, or part of it. Other times it disappeared from sight, but he knew where it was headed. In a good bit, making his way along a steep slope, he thought he saw movement on the back of a low hill close to the road. He tied the horse to a bush and used the binoculars. The distance was different from the last time he'd used them, and he had to adjust the screw. There was his lookout sure enough, a big man lying on his side on the back of the hill, a rifle beside him.

The man didn't move, so either he was asleep or lying very still. Morgan held the binoculars steady and waited, thinking it was time to get closer and see what the lookout was doing. What he didn't understand was why Fife had posted his son as a lookout. Heckwelder had been warned by telegraph, but there was no telegraph office in Beals Creek. Silver City had one, but no delivery boy would be sent forty miles, ten of them over a back country road, to deliver a message. No matter. He'd find out soon enough.

Morgan took one last look and saw the lookout sit up and drink from a bottle that he took from inside his shirt. Now he was able to get a clear look at the square face, the deep-set eyes. He couldn't see the hair because of the hat, didn't need to. The lookout—not much more than twenty—had to be Fife's son. He drank what was left in the bottle and threw it away, a dumb thing for a lookout to do. There were rocks there, but the bottle didn't break.

It could have, and sound carried.

He was on his back, his hat covering his face, when Morgan put the binoculars away and started down the slope. He had to find his way around a long gully choked with thornbush. That took time, but it was either that or be ripped in a dozen places. He got to the bottom of the hill where Fife's son was—what? Dozing from the whiskey or with eyes wide awake under the hat? Menzies said Fife could hold his liquor no matter how drunk he got, knew what he was doing, crazy though that might be. Like father, like son? No way to know that, not till he got close.

Morgan wondered if he could get around the hill, to try to come up from the other side. But that side would be just as hazardous and, for a few minutes at least, he wouldn't be able to see his man. It would be like fish in a barrel to shoot him as he was, but he couldn't do that. It would have to be the knife. Fuck it! One side of the hill was as bad as the other. He was wasting time.

Crumbling shale slid under his boots as he started the climb, and every pebble that rattled down behind him made too much noise. The sun was fierce and he sweated. It ran down his face and dripped from his chin, but he didn't raise his arm to sleeve it away. Any movement at all could give him away.

Now he was right below Fife's son and still moving. Only then did he draw the knife, and it was just clearing the scabbard when Fife's son roared and tried to come up off the ground, and nearly made it, before Morgan's full weight knocked him back and the knife buried itself in his heart. He would have screamed if Morgan's other hand hadn't clamped over his mouth and stayed there while he shuddered, shit in his pants, and died.

In the heat the smell was pretty bad. Morgan wiped his face and neck with his bandanna before he hunkered down beside the body. Too bad the bottle, glinting in the rocks, was empty. Fife's son looked younger dead.

Morgan found a clasp knife but no money. He hoped to find his old silver watch on one of these men. It was his father's watch and kept better time than the one he'd bought in Carson.

A dog started to bark far off and kept on barking as Morgan went to get his horse. He wondered if the dead man's shout had been heard. Maybe not. No way to tell what the dog was barking at. It could be him; it could be a teasing squirrel. But he decided it must be him when the barking didn't stop. Just the same, he had to go in there and finish the job. If Fife lit out he could lose him in the hills. Hunting a man in country that was familar to him would get Morgan nowhere, except maybe dead.

He got back on the road and headed in, leading the horse. A man on a horse made too good a target. The road twisted through hills that finally gave way to a small valley with a house and a small barn at the far end of it. The binoculars brought it close. What looked like a half Airedale was tied to the porch and barking its head off. The dog was big and looked half starved and as if it would come tearing out across the valley if it broke its rope.

A windmill for pumping well water turned slowly, driven by stray currents of air. There was no wind. Ten or twelve horses were in a corral, most of them lying down. Beyond a potato patch was a wire enclosure with cows nudging at baled hay.

He brought the binoculars back to the house. The door was open and a whiskey bottle stood to one side of it. Another bottle lay in front of the porch. The dog kept on throwing itself to the end of its rope. The binoculars were so good it was like the fucking brute was jumping in his face. He waited, holding the binoculars steady. Nobody came out to kick the dog quiet. Fife could be sleeping it off or silent behind a shotgun, watching the door.

The empty bottles said he was drunk, but if the stories were true that didn't mean much. But how much could any man drink before he went under. Thinking of Fife as a man who couldn't be downed was bullshit and no doubt a notion he liked to put out. Yes sir, Morgan thought, he had the right idea there, and pretty soon he'd know how true it was.

Riding straight across from where he was would make him easy pickings for a man with a rifle. He mounted and kicked the horse to a gallop, keeping to the north side of the valley. If Fife couldn't hear the dog he wouldn't hear the far-off hoofbeats. Morgan sure as hell could hear the dog. He rode right up to the side of the barn, got down, and tied the horse to a section of iron pipe lying in the weeds. He eased along the side of the barn to the door. No shots came at him, and the only sound was the dog barking. Now that he was so close the dog was getting crazier. He raised his gun and moved into the barn. At first, after the glare of the sun, he couldn't see a thing. Then Fife's voice said, "There is a cocked sawed-off aimed right at you. Drop the gun and step away from it."

Morgan could see now. Fife was behind a stack of hay bales, the sawed-off pointing over the top. All Morgan could see of Fife was his head and shoulders. He wasn't wearing a hat, and his gray-streaked black hair stood up wild and spiky. Morgan knew he'd been suckered by this so-called brainless drunk. He dropped the gun.

"Not so close," Fife warned him when he moved forward. "Stand there." The sawed-off didn't budge. "What in Christ's name are you doing here? Is a crack on the head and losing a few dollars that important to you? What do you think you're doing, you stupid bastard? We were watching for Van Wert; instead we get you. You must be crazy."

There was real surprise in Fife's growling voice. Anyway, why should he fake it when he had the gun? The instant the gun dropped from his hand Morgan braced himself for a double blast of buckshot that didn't come. Now he was still alive—for how long?—and Fife was talking. Not just talking, but inclined to talk.

For now he stayed where he was. "Answer me," he said.

Morgan didn't want to hurry his death by saying Margaret Deakin was the reason he was there. Maybe Fife didn't know she was dead. There would have been no need to warn him about Van Wert. News of the famous man catcher was in the paper, the talk of the saloons for a week before he showed up in Carson. Fife and his son were watching for Van Wert, not because they were sure he'd show up, but because he might.

"Don't be making up lies," Fife warned. "Talk quick."

"I thought I could get my father's watch back," Morgan said, thinking how Daniel Boone once got away from his redskin captors by flapping his arms and squawking like a turkey. So the story went.

Fife was no redskin. "That's a fucking load of shit."

"My father gave me the watch on his deathbed." Morgan didn't think much of that himself.

It made Fife laugh like a trained bear. Then his deep-set eyes got crafty: he was thinking. "It's the woman, isn't it? Can't be anything else. But we got no word you'd be traveling with a woman. Don't kill him we were told, only you got in the way, and I had to crack you one."

Morgan tried to say something.

Fife raised the sawed-off a little. "No questions from you, lame brain. You'll die not knowing a thing. You killed my son, didn't you?"

Morgan thought it was time to end it. No way he could get at the sawed-off. A twin blast of buckshot was better than what Fife was maybe thinking about. "I knifed the poxy bastard. I killed him like you made that woman on the stage kill herself. She cut her throat, you pea-brained, drunk, woman-killing son of a Scotch whore."

It didn't work. Fife just laughed at him. He had the power of life and death, and was enjoying himself. Men who people didn't respect were often like that when they got the upper hand. "I never did like that son of mine.

Dumb as the day is long. You got past him, didn't you? As for the woman I'm truly sorry to hear she killed herself. Wasn't nothing we did to her that wouldn't get right in time. She was, I tell you, one right juicy cunt. Man, the minute you fell down I was on her like a stallion. The way she tried to fight it. . . ."

It looked like Fife had done most of the work on Margaret Deakin. Morgan hated for it to end here.

Fife was laughing again. "A quick death is what you're hoping for, thickhead. A man would have to be thicker that you not to see that. Only it won't be quick, get it. I'm going to beat and kick you to death."

"Come ahead, you pig's prick," Morgan said. Maybe there was still a chance.

Fife came out holding the sawed-off. "You were thinking I'd lay down my gun so you could make a dive for yours. A stupid man might do that, not me." Fife seemed to be set on saying how dumb other people were. Dumb or smart didn't matter much here, Morgan thought. Fife scooped up Morgan's gun and knife and threw them far back into the barn. Then he set down the hammers of the sawed-off and stood it against the wall of the barn.

"You get your hands on that, you're welcome to it." He thought that was a funny notion and laughed at it. He moved toward Morgan, swinging his huge, scarred fists, five inches taller, more than a hundred pounds heavier. There was a big belly on him, not all of it whiskey bloat or overeating, and years of hard work had earned him muscles that hadn't sagged yet.

Fife stood where he was and waited for Morgan to come to him. His legs were spread apart and his fists swung like hammers. Otherwise he was still. Morgan knew he was slow on his feet—remembered from the change station—but he would have known without that. Fife began to edge forward. The sawed-off was right there, but Morgan didn't look at it. He knew Fife was daring him to try for a kick in the balls, the fastest way to blind an opponent with pain.

He made a kicking movement and Fife snapped his legs shut. He did it fast enough.

Fife raised his left hand and spat in it, then ground his two hands together, the saloon bully ready to take on all comers. He'd done it no end of times in tough towns from Calgary on down. "Dance all you like, bonehead. You're no Paddy Mack."

Morgan kicked him in the knee and he didn't even grunt. Too much meat there with the knee straight to do any damage. He raised his fists in front of him like a prizefighter, mocking the stance with a grin, but when he swung there was no skill in it. Morgan ducked the swing and hit him twice in the belly, and this time he grunted. He tried to get Morgan in a bear hug, but Morgan ducked down and got away from it.

Fife roared at him. "Duck and dodge, is that what you think? Come to Hamish, get it over with. Changed my mind—show mercy—I'll just snap your neck. *Crack!* You'll die quick, quicker than hanging." He stopped talking and rushed at Morgan with all the speed he could muster. Morgan knew he was dead if those huge hands got a grip on him. He dodged out of the way, but Fife managed to kick him in the side of the leg. It felt like he'd been hit full force with a pick handle, and he nearly went down. He made a rush for the sawed-off and got a blow in the back of the head that slammed him against the wall of the barn. White light danced in his head, and he hurt like hell.

"Yah! Yah!" Fife shouted and pretended to pick up the sawed-off, then he swung at Morgan and got him in the shoulder, and he was knocked backward, staggering until he regained his balance. He had taken three bad ones and hadn't done any damage. The next one he took could put him down for good and it would be all over. Fife kept laughing; the dog kept barking. Something about the way the dog kept on barking drove him crazy. He wondered if he should try to make a run for it. But if he ran—got out of the barn—Fife might be quick enough to blow his spine out with the sawed-off.

He circled, staying out of reach, but Fife didn't come after him right away. Instead he started going on about the dog. "Hear that dog out there! I'll just kill you, but that dog'll tear you to pieces. Maybe I'll let him have you before you die. Yes, sir. Yes, sir. I keep him hungry all the time, keep him on his mettle, yes, sir. He'd eat me if he could, only he's going to eat you, to tear your balls off and eat them."

Fife rushed again, and none of Morgan's blows got through. A wild swing from Fife didn't land right but was powerful enough to knock Morgan into a corner. The wind had been knocked out of him, but he didn't go down all the way, and the hurt would have been worse if he hadn't fallen against a sack of grain. The sack was open; he felt the powdery grain under his fingers. Fife was coming at him like a bull when he flung a handful of grain in the huge man's eyes. The dust did more damage than the grain, and Fife roared with anger and clawed at his eyes, but he couldn't stop his rush and his face hit the wall, and he was still turning when Morgan threw more grain and dust in his face and got out of the way. This time his legs were bent and he howled with pain as Morgan's boot tore off his kneecap. He stamped his foot as if that would drive the pain away.

Still howling and clawing at his eyes, trying to see, Fife tried another rush that carried him past Morgan. Morgan kicked him in the back of the bad knee and he howled louder. He started to fall, but righted himself before he did. Morgan tried for another knee kick, but missed. Fife wheeled his bulk around and came at Morgan again. This time there was no rush. He moved forward slowly with his hands out far in front of him, relying on his size to push Morgan back against the wall where he could grab his neck and get a choke hold, at the same time battering Morgan's head against the wood. Suddenly one of his hands closed into a fist and shot out straight with tremendous force. It hit Morgan in the forehead and his back hit the wall, bounced off the wood, throwing him. Morgan was down on his hands and knees, his head spinning, and Fife was trying to land a kick that would end it. Morgan took a kick in the thigh that would have been worse if he hadn't been scrambling up when it landed. But the pain was bad and the leg felt numb, and he didn't know if he'd be able to stand when he got all the way up. One more kick like that, only harder, and Fife would have him. The kick came, but didn't land.

Fife threw himself forward like a falling tree and tried to bury Morgan with his weight. His huge body hit the floor of the barn and shook it. His clawing hands nearly got Morgan's legs, but by then Morgan was up and running for the sawed-off. Morgan's hands closed around the sawed-off and he spun around, trying to stand right on the damaged leg. He was thumbing back the twin hammers, his hands shaking, and Fife was up on his feet and coming at him again. Fife's last rush carried him right up to the muzzle of the sawed-off.

Morgan stuck the sawed-off in his belly and squeezed both triggers. Muffled by flesh, the sawed-off made a double whomping sound, and Fife folded in two.

Morgan went to look for his gun and knife.

Chapter Ten

The dog broke its rope and came bounding at Morgan before he could get close to the porch. He was still stunned by the fight, and for an instant, all he could do was shake his head, trying to clear it. The dog was right on top of him before he pulled his gun and killed the damn thing with three bullets. It dropped at his feet and lay there quivering. Killing the dog reminded him that he would have to turn the stock loose before he left.

Inside the house was surprisingly neat, with none of the mess you'd expect with a brute like Fife, no half-eaten plates of food lying around, no dirty underpants hanging from doorknobs, no empty cans. There were two rooms: a main room and a sleeping room with two beds in it, one a real factory bed, the other a homemade shelf bed nailed to the wall. Against the other wall was a chest of drawers with nothing in the top drawer but papers. Morgan looked in the bottom drawer and found nothing but folded shirts, long johns, and underpants.

He spread the papers on Fife's bed and looked through

them. There was Fife's discharge from the British Canadian Army. Honorable, it said. A lot of letters addressed to places in British Columbia, none to anyplace in Nevada, written by Mrs. Flora Fife. Nothing there. He turned over an advertising flyer for the Butterfield Nevada Stage Line. Still dazed by the beating he'd taken, Morgan had to read it twice. The McHargville division needed drivers, guards, station agents, and hostlers. They were paying good wages for the right men. Anyone interested should apply in person to Mr. Theron Vail, the division superintendent.

Morgan folded the flyer and put it in his pocket. He wondered if Fife had applied for a job and been turned down, as Tobe Canty was. He might have. Menzies had turned him down for a job. But the flyer by itself didn't have to mean anything. Years after the first big silver strike, when the big companies were getting their grip on everything, it was hard to get men to work at steady jobs in Nevada. These flyers put out by undermanned companies were everywhere, and who was this Theron Vail? Frank C. Eaton was the man in charge of the McHargville division. His name was on the sign over the door. There was no date on the flyer so it could be old. Vail could have been fired, transferred, or dead. Jesus Christ! he thought. God didn't open the first door unless the second was nailed shut.

He found his father's silver watch in a box of shotgun cartridges, and that was the only thing that cheered him up. No matter how hard he looked he found nothing that tied Hamish Fife to anything except the wandering life he'd led since he left Calgary. He looked at his watch. The day was wearing on. Time to let the stock run and get out of there.

Buzzards were already at work when he rode past the hill where Fife's son lay dead. The fight with Fife had taken a lot out of him, and he was tired, sore all over, but mostly tired. It seemed a long time since Idaho. Going out to the main road he wondered if anybody had heard the shots that killed the dog. Not too likely. Sooner or later they'd find what was left of the Fifes. Fife's reputation as a dangerous man might keep them out for a while, but some hardy souls would venture in there, if only to see what they could steal. He hoped to be a long way off before they did.

There was another fair-sized town about forty or fifty miles down the road. Something like that. He remembered waking up and looking at it from the stage while they changed the horses. Towns and camps were stretched out all along the McHargville road. There was gambling in the big places, and he wondered if Heckwelder might be drawn into a game by his craze for cards or whatever it was. It wasn't likely that Heckwelder sweated while the roulette wheel turned. You could lose your money too quickly at roulette, and it wasn't a gentleman's game. Poker would be Heckwelder's game, with the idea he had of himself as a steely eyed Southern gentleman gambler raking in big pots.

The stretch of road was bad, torn up by hundreds of heavy ore wagons coming and going, and at times he had to walk the horse. If the gelding broke a leg he'd be left in the middle of nowhere with no money to buy another horse, even if he could find one. He could walk to the next town, but what would he do then? He didn't know if they still hung horse thieves in Nevada, and he didn't want to find out.

His belly reminded him that he hadn't eaten since the day before. After he grained and watered the horse he opened a can and ate the food cold. He craved coffee but went without, thinking he'd boil up a pot when he made camp for the night. By late afternoon, after he'd traveled about twenty miles, he caught up with a wagon and asked the driver how far the next town was. The man said about thirty-five miles and gave him a queer look when he asked what it was called. "Limerick City," the man said. "Used to be Silver City, but that name was taken by two other towns, so they changed it."

That night, lying in his blankets, he tried to figure what he'd do if he found Heckwelder in a game. That wasn't too likely, but it could happen. By now Heckwelder might think himself safe enough to risk a game, as a far-gone drunk might risk going on a bender, even at the cost of his life. His wife was a determined woman, and Morgan could be dead by now. Morgan knew he was thumbing the scales here. He knew some things about Heckwelder, but that was far from knowing the whole man. He would have to wait and see. Lord how tired he was of telling himself to wait and see.

He got to Limerick City after nightfall the next day. The punishment he got from Fife was catching up real good, and it hurt bad just to get down from the horse. A long soak in a hot tub would help some, and maybe he'd do that later. He stabled the horse and got something to eat before he started making the rounds of the saloons. Limerick City was lively but not big enough to have regular gambling halls, and all the tables and wheels were in the back of saloons.

He started with one and went on to another, and by the time he got to the next to last, Mike Malone's Irish House, he still hadn't found Heckwelder. Dude gambler, about forty, pale face, waxed mustache, that's what he kept looking for. One man looked something like that, but he was far too old, at least past sixty, and when he left the game it was with a woman who came looking for him.

He wondered if Heckwelder had enough money left from the robbery to get into a private game in a hotel. He asked one of the bartenders, and the man said, "No private games in this town, mister. What you see is what there is."

He was tired of looking in saloons and not finding anything, and hoping to find Heckwelder gambling was a dumb idea. It was still early, and he could put some miles behind him before he quit. He was thinking about that while finishing his beer. Ready to go, he heard a commotion in the street. It sounded like a loud wedding party or a quiet lynching. A lot of laughing and yelling, then a whole bunch of men trooped into the saloon, led by a short woman with flaming red hair. She went right up to the bar and slapped down some paper money and yelled at the bartender closest to her. "Clem, you old son of a bitch! I thought you were dead. Since you ain't how's about setting up some suds for my friends."

"You're a card, Kate," the bartender said. "Hey, Kate!" the other bartender called from the far end of the bar. The bartenders perked up, everybody perked up. Morgan had never seen so many people perking up at one time. No way to tell what she was? Wayward daughter of a rich mine owner? The most popular madam in town? But she didn't look like that or anything else he could think of. Then the proprietor came out from where the games were and shook hands with her.

"How's the newspaper business, Katie dear?" he said.

She slapped him on the arm and buried her face in a mug of beer. "Couldn't be better, you old rascal," she said, wiping the foam off her mouth with the back of her hand. "Mike's serves the best beer in Nevada, I always say."

An old man nudged Morgan. "That's Kate O'Hara, works for the Carson City paper. Things hum when she's around. Always good for a drink and a laugh." The old man picked up his free beer. Morgan got one too, but he didn't want it.

The few bills she'd put on the bar were long drunk up. No more were put in their place. The proprietor nodded to the bartenders to set up another round. Good for business, Morgan thought, but that would be the end of the free beer. The second round disappeared and men were clamoring to pay for their own beer. Kate O'Hara joked and laughed, calling some of the men by their names, asking how things were, if they'd struck it rich yet? Morgan saw she was smacking her lips over her second beer, but not drinking much of it. Over the top of her mug she was watching him.

It quieted down a bit and she pushed her way close to him. "You're not drinking your beer," she said.

A man came up and shook hands with her before Morgan could answer.

"Thanks for the beer," Morgan said, and drank some of it.

"You're Morgan, aren't you?" she said, not waiting for an answer. "I've been looking for you all the way from Carson. I was over the line in California, didn't hear what happened till I got back. Inquest was over, and you were gone. In case you didn't get my name right I'm Kate O'Hara and I'm a reporter for the—"

"I heard, Miss O'Hara."

"Kate! Kate! You ever hear of me?"

"No." Morgan drank some beer.

"You will. You're hearing from me now. Used to work in Chicago, but that town's been getting tame since the O'Learys burned it down."

"I thought the cow did it."

"Don't you believe it. Mike O'Leary did it for the insurance."

"He insured the entire city?" Morgan knew where this was leading, but he was enjoying the bullshit.

"Just the part he owned," Kate O'Hara said, enjoying it herself. "The fire got out of hand, see. I had proof, but they wouldn't print it—*men!*"

"You don't like men?"

"I love the bastards. I'd love them more if they weren't so worried about their balls. They're so proud of having them they worry about losing them. You're not worried, are you?"

"No. But I'd like to keep them as long as I could."

That got a short laugh. Morgan knew she was ready to get down to business. This was the first time a reporter had come to him for anything, and if it had been a man. . . .

But this one surely wasn't a man. No cigarette-stained mustache; no beer on his breath. Beer breath she had—but what a difference. Green eyes went with the red hair, and the shirt. The coat and whipcord pants she wore didn't do much to hide her figure. The pants weren tight enough to say come and get it, not that the cut made much difference with women so scarce in Nevada.

A leather-covered notebook stuck out of the deep pocket of her coat. Morgan half expected her to draw it like a pistol. Instead she said, "I read the inquest report, what you testified to, and I talked to Malley and his deputies. Malley likes to keep on my good side, but didn't tell me much. He did say he could well understand why you'd want to bring these men to justice. Does that mean you intend to kill them, never mind the legalities?"

"Malley didn't say that, did he?"

"He didn't say it, but he hinted at it. Malley is full of hints, which is not all he's full of. But he's a smart old villain."

"Why should I tell you anything?" Morgan said. "Anything I might say you'd twist anyway. Your paper said I lost ten thousand dollars."

She laughed. "I had nothing to do with that. I was away, remember? Anyway, what's so terrible about it? Makes the story more interesting. Ninety dollars is not too interesting. But you can believe me, anything I report will be the truth. I'll make sure they write it right."

"You don't write it yourself?"

"I'm not in the office much. Getting the facts is more my job. How can you get a big story sitting around on your ass? I send my stuff in by telegraph or the next stage. Crowley the editor fixes it up. Does that answer your question?"

"No, it doesn't. I asked you what do I gain by talking to you?"

She gave him a sharp look. "Most people like to talk to reporters if they have nothing to hide. It's a reporter's duty to get at the truth. The people have a right to know. You think that's funny, do you?"

"It's not my duty to help sell newspapers." Morgan thought that was a good one. She was getting mad. Maybe he shouldn't get her too mad. Maybe she could tell him things he didn't know. Reporters usually knew where the shit was buried. "But I'll answer your questions if you'll answer mine. Tit for tat."

"Tits to you," she said. "You've got yourself a deal." She looked around. "But this is no place to talk. The walls have ears."

Morgan didn't see any ears, but he did spot a few hard-ons. There was hardly a man there that didn't want to fuck her. No shame or blame attached to that. She wasn't candy-box pretty but good looking in a lively, bawdy way. The town had whores but after all a whore was just a paid hole and this was a real woman. Some of the men sneaking looks at her or admiring her openly weren't aware of their hard-ons. Others, the shy ones, did their best to hide the bone in their pants.

Morgan was still thinking about it. He didn't want to go through a lot of bullshit. Answering questions and getting nothing but bullshit in return. He didn't think of himself as one of those men who tried to keep women in their places. As long as they took their rightful place in bed a woman could do as she damn well pleased outside of it. Which didn't mean that he was ready to jump every time they snapped their fingers. Shake their asses—that was a different matter. His hard-on told him to get a move on.

Kate O'Hara said the same thing. "You want to bring a bottle along?" When he said no she told the bartender to put ten bottles of beer in a sack. Morgan knew he was a well-hated man when he went out with her.

"I already checked in," she said at the hotel. "If I didn't find you I wanted to get a good night's sleep. That's what I've been doing, trying to catch up to you during the day, sleeping in hotels if there was one. One night I slept in a stable. Camping out is not for me."

They got upstairs and she stretched out on the bed, saying, "Ah Christ, it's good to get my backside onto something soft. I'll never get used to all that horseback riding. The only horses I knew back in Chicago were dray horses. Uncork me a beer like a good fella."

Morgan gave it to her. He got one for himself and put it on the floor beside his chair. The bed was looking better all the time, and so was she. If she didn't want to be fucked maybe he could get some sleep. Sleeping out was all right if you had to do it, but there was nothing like a warm bed on a bitter cold Nevada night.

"Anything you can tell me about these robberies? I just know what I said at the inquest." Morgan reached down for his bottle.

Kate O'Hara sat up. "Let us not be jumping the gun. I'm the reporter here. What can you tell me that you didn't say? Like, for instance, did you really have to kill Tobe Canty?"

"I did. Really and truly. I was cleared. I want to stay cleared. You're asking me to admit to murder. Why look for trouble?"

She pulled at her beer. "For my own information I'd like to know. I'd like to know what kind of a man I'm dealing with."

"I had to kill him." Morgan drank a mouthful of Mike's beer. It was not the best beer in Nevada.

"What you tell me won't be repeated outside this room." There was a lot of sincerity in her voice. "It need not be. I can use my discretion. Crowley doesn't have to know everything I know."

Morgan had to smile at her. "Then you're a rotten reporter. Forget Tobe Canty. Can we move on to something else?"

"All right. If you won't, you won't. I was hoping you'd trust me. In Silver City you were asking questions about a man who calls himself Buford De Forest. That's a phony if ever I heard one. What about it? You think he's one of the robbers?"

Morgan had to think before he answered. The man at the Silver City Stables Company and the telegraph clerk could tie him in to Heckwelder, known to them as De Forest. And there was a chance that the hotel clerk hadn't been sleeping as soundly as he let on. Any way he looked at it, one or all three could tie him in.

"He might be," Morgan said.

"Jesus Christ! If you don't think he is—The hotel clerk says Mrs. De Forest was up in your room for hours, and when she finally did come down, she was like a bat out of hell. What was she doing? Trying to bribe you with her body? And were you bribed, and did you double-cross the lady?"

"We just talked," Morgan said. "I tried to convince her that her husband would be better off giving himself up. It took a long time."

"Ha, ha! But you finally did convince her? What did you hope she'd do? Lead you to her husband?"

Morgan set his beer down. "I thought she might do that."

"Then why did you wait till morning to go after her? The clerk said you came down much later."

"All right. I didn't think she'd lead me anywhere at three in the morning. Or any time. Did you talk to her?"

"Yes I talked to her. Of course I talked to her. She denied being at the hotel, denied knowing you, denied everything. It was laughable to even think her husband might be connected in some way with these robberies. She laughed when she said it. I know liars, and she's a good one. Insisted her husband was on a business trip. Did you fuck her?"

"We just talked," Morgan said.

"If you didn't you could have. That woman would do anything for Buford. I don't know that I'd ever do that for a man." Kate O'Hara tilted her bottle as she thought about it. I'd fuck a man to get a good story—I have done it—but to do it for—At this point I must tell you, you won't get my drawers off unless you come up with some answers. Otherwise, dear heart, you can pull it."

Morgan muttered something.

"Don't sulk," she said, rolling around on the bed until her feet were sticking out. "Pull my boots off, will you? I'm too tired to do it myself. I've been on that goddamned horse for what feels like a thousand miles."

"About a hundred and eighty. Why should your feet hurt?"

"It's not my feet, it's my backside. At Beal's Creek you asked about a man named Hamish Fife. The saloon keeper told me on no account to go to Fife's ranch, or whatever it is. Told me he was a brute, a real savage, and it wasn't safe. The man said Van Wert had been at his place before you got there, but didn't ask about Fife, he'd wanted only to talk to you. What does it mean? Did you talk to either of them?"

Morgan said, "I decided Fife could wait. One of the robbers was a big man, a big bear of a man with what sounded like a Scotch accent. Somebody gave me a tip that Fife fitted that description. Then I heard he was a hard-working man that seldom left his place. Didn't seem likely he was a stage robber."

"No more than the tinhorn gambler was." Kate O'Hara turned on her side so she could look at Morgan. "You're a bad liar, and you're making me mad. Here's what I think happened. You killed Canty. You would have killed De Forest, but he got away from you. You probably killed this Hamish Fife. I can't be sure about that, but I can find out."

Morgan got a bad feeling. "You could do that. You could get hold of Van Wert and let him find out. And somebody could stop you."

Fear flickered in her eyes, but she tried to hide it. "I have no such notion, Morgan. I'm not sure why you're doing this, but anything you do to those men is all right with me. The things they did to that woman. Is it because of her?"

Morgan didn't think he had a whole lot to lose. By the time it was over, if he lived that long, Van Wert wouldn't have much trouble pinning the killings on him. "Somebody has to make it right for her," he said. Suddenly he was angry. "What the fuck do you care what happened to her? Just another story for your fucking rag. Fuck you and fuck Van Wert, I'll get it done."

She jumped off the bed and blocked the door before he could get out. Now she was as angry as he was. She hit him in his sore belly and it hurt. He grabbed her by both arms before she could hit him again.

"I'll fucking murder you," she said, trying to get her arms free. "You big stupid horseshit horse rancher! What the fuck do you know about me? I was sick when I heard about that woman. You think I don't care, is that what you think? Just another story for my fucking rag? If you think that, you don't know me at all."

Morgan let her go. "I guess I talked out of turn. Know you? How in hell could I know you? This is going nowhere. I better—"

She pushed him away from the door. "Sit down and drink your beer. Look here, Morgan, I'm not the mothering kind, but it looks to me like you need a friend. What happened with this woman that set you off so? I'm not asking as a reporter, you hear me."

Morgan told it simply, and when he finished, Kate O'Hara kept nodding her head. "It's craziness, but I think I understand it and I'll help you if I can. Nothing we can do about it right this minute. You look tired. I know I'm tired. You want to go to bed and talk later?"

"Might not be a bad idea," Morgan said.

But once they were naked under the covers his tiredness went away. Most of the tiredness had been in his head, the snooping around, all the roundabout talk, not being able to trust anybody. He wasn't one for trusting people who hadn't earned trust, and even as his hands moved over Kate O'Hara's body, he wasn't sure he trusted her, no matter what she'd said. Wanting to trust somebody was the quickest way to get euchred. Sincerity, the appearance of it, was this woman's stock in trade. The hell with all that! He'd fuck her and see what happened.

She talked tough, but not in bed, and her hands were as gentle as her voice. Her legs were wide open and her cunt was sopping wet, ready to receive him, and she gave a low moan as he thrust into her. Her hands were small but strong and they gripped his ass tightly, pulling him deeper inside her. She was a small woman, but she took the full length of his cock with ease.

"Kiss me! Please kiss me," she murmured, and when he kissed her hard, her tongue pushed its way into his mouth and he sucked on it and her cunt tightened and relaxed as if it felt his sucking. That was more like it, no more questions. So many questions and such a temper. He liked her better in bed, her tongue in his mouth, her hands clutching at him. There was a lot of energy in this pint-sized woman and she moved freely under him in spite of his weight. After days on the road she smelled of sweat and hay—that would be the stable—and that was fine with him. Soon the smell of sex would be stronger than the other smells, and that was even better. More than anything else she liked him to draw back nearly all the way, then hold it there for an instant before driving it in to the hilt. Every time he pulled his cock back and hesitated she raised her ass, bracing herself for the thrust, and then she gasped as if he'd driven the breath from her lungs. He knew she was building up to a climax when she took her hand away from his ass and squeezed her breast so the nipple stuck up, wanting him to suck it. His lips tweaked at her nipple, and he quickened his thrusts. No hesitation now: his cock went in and out of her relentlessly, and fast. It was moving even faster when she sucked in a great breath of air and came while she was blowing it out. He kept on shafting her as she came, holding her steady with big hands, giving it to her with all his strength.

"Come! Come!" she begged him. "Come! Fill me with hot, sticky come. I want to feel it spurting out of you . . . your juice shooting out of you into me . . . get it all into me . . . get your balls into me . . . I can feel it starting . . . let it go, let it go. . . ."

Morgan started to come, and she jerked and twisted under him. It was a long come and it made him shudder, but she didn't want him to stop. She came again and again, and when everything was drained out of him, he pushed his finger into her cunt and stroked her come-slick knob; he thought she was going to explode. "Jesus! Oh Jesus!" she cried out. "I can't stand it, I'm going out of my head!" And then she reached the very peak of pleasure and collapsed.

Morgan couldn't remember a woman who'd relaxed so completely. Others had faked it, for his sake and out of pride, but this was the real thing. They lay side by side, and she seemed to be in no mood to talk. That was all right, no good rushing her with questions. But he still wanted her to keep up her part of the deal. To give him the information he needed, and if what she told him was of no value, then he'd have to keep on going as he was.

"Morgan," she murmured, as if reading his mind. "You mind if we talk after I get some sleep? I'm all worn out, honest I am. We'll talk, honest we will." Her voice trailed off and she began to snore.

Tired, still aching, Morgan felt himself drifting off.

Chapter Eleven

They rassled again while it was still dark, and first light was glimmering in the room by the time they finished. Well rested and full of energy, Kate O'Hara was ready to start the day. "Up and at 'em," she said, bouncing her ass off the bed. "We'll get a quick breakfast at Lanty's and be on our way."

Morgan started to get dressed. "You wouldn't be forgetting something, by any chance?"

Kate O'Hara buttoned her pants and pulled on her boots. "We'll talk on the road. That way you won't be tempted to leave me behind."

Morgan had been thinking just that, and she seemed to know it. Still, he could always leave her on the road, as bad a rider as she said she was. It would be a mean thing to do, but he had to look out for himself.

"All right," he said. "Let's get some breakfast."

Lanty's was an all-night beaner jammed with miners coming off a shift. Morgan didn't think the tired miners, Cornishmen and Irishmen, would have the smallest interest in what she told him. Some of them knew her from the saloons and they were glad to see her. Morgan ate in silence, wanting to get started.

Kate O'Hara's mount was an old, docile cow pony, about her size and speed, Morgan thought. They started out through the waking town, and she got more waves and hellos. "When you goin' to put my name in the paper?" one man yelled at her. "Soon as you start using your real one," she yelled back. The man laughed. Morgan didn't.

Out past the town she said, "If you leave me I'll follow you anyway. I'll haunt you, get it. You have to swear you won't."

"I swear," Morgan said.

She considered that for a while. "All right. You say Menzies hired a lawyer to look into Butterfield's business affairs. What you don't know is he hired Charles W. Fallon. Now Charles W. Fallon isn't just any lawyer. He used to be a real bigshot back in Albany, New York, before he came here by way of several other towns. There were rumors that he bribed a juror in a murder trial, but the man conveniently fell into the river and drowned before the district attorney could get at him. You'd think that would have taught him a lesson, but no. Less than a year later he was accused of stealing big money from an elderly, senile client, and this time he fled before they could dig deeper. It's said that some of the friends in the state legislature helped to bury the investigation. Nice fella, am I right?"

Morgan knew she expected him to say something. "Sounds like it."

"Well, anyway. News of his crooked dealings followed him out here after he'd finally set up in McHargville. That was about two years ago. Respectable people shy away from him, but he's got no shortage of clients, far from it. Criminals come to him as first choice when they get their dicks in the wringer. Fallon is a very smart lawyer, but an absolute crook. You get the picture?"

"It makes sense that Menzies would want the smartest lawyer around." Morgan was thinking about Menzies, so open and honest, it seemed like.

Kate O'Hara gave out with a humorless laugh. "You think he needed Fallon just to poke around. Well maybe he did. But Fallon doesn't come cheap, so Menzies had to have a real interest. But here's the part I've been saving. Fallon defended Menzies at his manslaughter trial in Albany. That's right—Albany. Fallon nearly got him off, but the evidence was too strong. In spite of Fallon's eloquence the fact remained that Menzies beat a much smaller man to death. Some rival moonshiner. They got to fighting over who owned which mountain."

That was a new one for Morgan, running moon in upstate New York. "Not much of a crime, moonshining," he said. "Hardly puts Menzies in the same class as the James Gang. Menzies told me the thing he feared most was going back to prison."

Kate O'Hara cursed her old pony for stumbling in a rough patch. Morgan told her not to hold the reins so tightly. "Of course he doesn't want to go back, what else would he say? You don't know ex-jailbirds like I do. You can't let yourself be taken in by these birds."

No more than by newspaper reporters, Morgan thought. But there could be something in what she said. "You want to go back and talk to Menzies, not that it'll do any good."

Kate O'Hara's pony was moving better in the wagon ruts. "I think we should go ahead and talk to Fallon. He's like Malley in a way, will talk and talk and say nothing. But it might shake him up a little, not that he'll show it."

"You know him?"

"I know everybody. I interviewed him, sort of, when news of his shady past leaked this far west. But I didn't go in empty handed. First I got Crowley to check with the Pinkertons in Albany. Lord, how he squawked at the expense! But it was worth it. How do you think I know so much? As you can imagine, he was quite indignant. If they had any proof of their accusations, why wasn't he disbarred, why wasn't he in jail? The entire thing was a tissue of lies woven by his political enemies back in Albany. He used the word dastardly. We wrote him up in the paper, and he threatened to sue, but didn't."

"Watch that hole," Morgan said. She wasn't keeping her eye on the road. "Why would he want to talk to you after that?"

She got her pony safely around the hole. "To get some idea what I'm up to, and if you're still thinking about leaving me, keep this in your scheming mind. Fallon may not want to talk to you. To him you'd be no more than a small potatoes horse rancher from Idaho, that is, if he doesn't know who you are. But I represent the power of the press. I can get more out of him than you can."

"That's what you think." Morgan wished they could move a little faster. "I could make him talk."

Kate O'Hara laughed at that. "You're wrong there, my friend. Fallon is no odd-job man like Tobe Canty. For all his smelly reputation Fallon gets on fine with the McHargville marshal and besides that he's got some very bad lads at his beck and call. Former and future clients. You get rough with Fallon, and they'll bury you."

"All right," Morgan said. "You talk to him." That's what he said, but he hadn't made up his mind yet. If Fallon was as smart and slippery as she said, what could she hope to get out of him? Probably nothing. But maybe it was better than taking on Fallon cold.

They rode on with Kate O'Hara doing most of the talking. There wasn't much more to be said about Fallon so she started on Menzies. What did he mean by saying Scotchmen weren't generally known as crooks and lawbreakers? Look at Boss Tweed, she said, Scotch on both sides and the biggest crook in the world. They were craftier than other crooks, that's all, and when it came to pure greed they were slicker than Yankee traders.

Ten miles out Morgan said it was time to water the horses, let them rest. They sat on a rock beside the road and Kate O'Hara drank water. It was hot as hell and Morgan drank some himself. Lord, but it would be good to get back to Idaho, where the sun could be hot, but didn't fry your eyeballs. In the high country it was green and cool, especially in the morning, and you weren't sweating by seven o'clock.

"You know, I'm going to be the first female war correspondent," Kate O'Hara said. She wet a handkerchief and rubbed at the dust on her face. "I have it all mapped out. After I make a name for myself in Carson—after all, it is the state capitol—I'll go to San Francisco, and then to New York. That's where the real newspapers are. I'll write stories that'll make their hair stand on end. I'll fuck Gordon Bennett Junior—they say he's a horny bastard. I'll fuck him silly if I have to, and then I'm off to the wars."

Morgan knew nothing about the newspaper business or how it worked. "Good luck to you," he said, thinking she had the balls to do it, if such a thing could be said about a woman. All over the country women were demanding their rights and why shouldn't they? Women made life worth living.

A long way after that they saw a horse by the side of the road. "That horse looks dead," Kate O'Hara said when Morgan got down to make sure it was. Morgan looked at the horse. "It's been dying for a long time, but it isn't dead." He drew his gun and shot the horse. It had been a good horse and he wondered what kind of miserable son of a bitch would leave a broken-legged animal to die like that. Then he saw the brand half blotted by dust and stooped down to examine it. SCS. Silver City Stables. Heckwelder, who else could it be? It didn't have to be, but he thought it was. Only a bollixed-up useless piece of shit would leave a horse to die like that.

Kate O'Hara wanted to know what was going on and didn't take it kindly when he told her to shut up. So he had to tell her again. The rifle scabbard was empty so the bastard had taken the rifle and canteens and gone on ahead, leaving the horse to die. All that dust on the horse, it could have been lying there for a day, maybe more. There was no way to be sure. It could have been two full days.

He mounted up and told Kate O'Hara what he thought. "This is the horse Heckwelder—"

"Who the hell is Heckwelder?"

"That's De Forest's real name."

Kate O'Hara wanted a lot more. "What else are you hiding, Morgan? Suddenly De Forest turns out to be Heckwelder. You're not telling me the whole truth."

"What about you? You know more than you're saying. The hell with it. He's up ahead of us somewhere, walking or riding in a wagon. Either way it'll be slow going, so let's be moving."

"You're the one standing around jabbering." Kate O'Hara kicked her pony and rode ahead, but Morgan caught up with her before she'd gone far.

"Ease up," he said. "You saw what happened to that horse back there. Keep this up and you'll be afoot or dead of a broken neck. I won't carry you double. Now quit your talking and look where you're going. Heckwelder has a rifle and knows how to use it, so his wife says."

"She'd say anything, you yokel." Kate O'Hara was still mad at him.

She could be right about that, Morgan thought. Anyway, it wasn't likely that they'd catch up with Heckwelder this side of McHargville. Walking or riding, he was sure to be far ahead. At McHargville he could catch a long-distance stage to Salt Lake and points east, and when he got to a railroad he could disappear for good. Morgan didn't know how far he'd follow him if that happened.

Too soon to be making decisions like that.

McHargville was sixty miles or so from Limerick City, and they had gone half that distance by late afternoon. No mining camps had sprouted up between the two towns. No silver, no mining. Except for the telegraph line running along beside the road, the country looked as desolate and empty as it must have looked a hundred years before. The hot wind blew up hard, thick with dust. Morgan's horse was holding up fine, but the pony was beginning to falter. The poor animal should be put out to pasture or sent to the glue factory, he thought but didn't say. Kate O'Hara was in a sullen mood.

It was getting dark when they came to a ramshackle trading post standing by itself, no shacks clustered close by, nothing but the store. The place couldn't have been more than thirty years old, and already it was falling down and tin beer signs had been used to cover the holes in the front wall. The porch steps had crumbled, and they had to climb up a plank to get inside.

Dust was thick on everything, and the single oil lamp didn't give much light. One side had hardware, the other canned goods and bottled beer, plug tobacco and sourballs. A cold stove stood between the two counters and the man sitting at it got up when they came in. He had a flat, clean-shaven face and a flat voice.

"Never heard of you," he said when Kate O'Hara said who she was. Morgan didn't say. "Don't stock newspapers and don't read 'em. Full of lies. You want to buy something?"

Morgan answered for Kate O'Hara, who looked miffed. "Two bottles of that beer should do it." The price was high, but he paid it, then asked about Heckwelder.

The storekeeper wasn't unfriendly, just flat voiced, matter of fact. "No need to describe him nor why you want him. Come in here about this time last night, all tired and dirty, wanting to buy a horse, said his own broke a leg way back. Well I didn't like his looks—gambler trash—

and I said I couldn't help him. Then he said what about that mule out there, and I told him it wasn't for sale at any price. Well then he offered me five times what any mule is worth and when I said no—I love that mule—he sort of looked like he was going to take it anyway. He had a pistol and a rifle, but I had this"—the storekeeper took a .38 caliber double action from his pants pocket—"and that ended the conversation. Would you be wanting anything else in the grocery line?"

"Dumb son of a bitch," Kate O'Hara said when they got outside. "No wonder he doesn't read newspapers. He can't read. That, or he's just plain ignorant."

Lord, how she could carry on. "It's not so bad," Morgan said. "Heckwelder's less than a day ahead of us, not that much. If he hasn't found a horse he'll be limping pretty badly by now. We'll find a place for the night and start out early. He must be getting desperate to think of robbing that tough bird in there."

Still miffed, Kate O'Hara said, "I don't think he's so tough."

"Pretty tough," Morgan said. "Only a fool like Heckwelder would think of taking him on. That means he's desperate."

They made camp in a hollow out of the wind, and that's all you could say for it. Morgan grained the animals while Kate O'Hara made coffee. After they ate and the horses were secured for the night they rolled up in their blankets. It got cold and Kate O'Hara crawled in with Morgan, and it was the first time in a long time that he fucked a woman on the hard ground. The horses fretted at the sounds coming from the blankets, but they got used to it because it went on for so long. Out here Kate O'Hara could let herself so, and she screamed every time she came. But the night was wearing on, and after her third or fourth climax she said they ought to get some sleep. Morgan opened one of the bottles of beer, and she was asleep before she finished it. He covered her and drank the rest of the beer and lay back feeling all right. All the fucking seemed to be doing his sore muscles a lot of good. They would probably catch up with Heckwelder the next day, and that would be one man closer to the end. He had killed three of them and couldn't say it made him feel any better. Maybe it wasn't supposed to. He knew he could live with anything else he had to do.

They were back on the road by five o'clock. At that hour, in the gray light, it was still bitter cold and Kate O'Hara rode with a blanket draped over her shoulders. Morgan didn't bother with that. Soon it would be hot enough to fry an egg on a flat rock. The sun came up full and Kate O'Hara put away the blanket and drank the second bottle of beer. By seven o'clock they were about eight miles from where they'd started. Kate O'Hara was saying that she'd probably write a book about her experiences as a war correspondent.

They were starting up a long hill and she was still talking about the book. A rifle cracked from somewhere up above, and Morgan felt the burn of a bullet along his side under his left arm. His horse spooked and threw him hard, and he was trying to get up when the rifle cracked again and Kate O'Hara pitched off her pony. More bullets came at him as he crawled close and saw she was dead, shot through the chest. His horse had run off the road and was now running back, wild eyed with panic. Another bullet came close as he grabbed the saddle horn and hung from the galloping horse until he was able to swing into the saddle.

He didn't mean to charge up the hill, but that's where the panicked horse was taking him, and even as he tried to control the animal he knew he could go down if he tried too hard. Bullets rattled like hail, and the horse was taking him right into the storm of lead. The hidden rifleman was firing as fast as he could work the loading lever. He saw the shape of a man and the sun coming off a rifle barrel, then it was gone, but the shooting didn't stop. The horse ran on fast and wild and that was giving the shooter a bad target and keeping Morgan from being hit. He had the horse under some control now, but didn't try to slow it much. . . .

There was no cover beside the road, just up above to one side of it, where the shooter was. It was all going so fast he didn't know if it was Heckwelder up there. The shooting slackened and he thought maybe he could get past the shooter and come at him from behind. Another two bullets were loosed at him, and then the shooting stopped—maybe the shooter was running down to the road to try for a better shot. He galloped over the top of the hill. . . .

So many bullets had been fired at him he couldn't keep count. The shooter up there was using something like a 15-shot Henry. No other rifle took so many bullets, but maybe he was reloading now. With an old Henry you could reload all at once just by pushing in a tube with fifteen bullets in it. If he ran into that much lead close up he'd have to be hit. One thought after another raced through Morgan's mind. One made sense, and one didn't, and the horse was moving faster than he could think. . . .

The shooter hadn't opened up again and suddenly the top of the hill looked like the wrong place to be. He got the horse off the road without a fall, and it galloped along a line of rocks down from where the shooter was. If the shooter wasn't there he was running to a new position, maybe already in it and lining up for a killing shot. . . .

Morgan reined in the horse just enough so he wouldn't be hurt when he grabbed the Winchester from the scabbard and rolled off. The horse was coming under his control, and he was making himself a better target, but there was nothing else to do. Still no bullets came, and he pulled back on the reins, snatched up the Winchester and let himself drop into a dip with brush and sand in it. But it wasn't all sand and the rocks underneath punished his already bruised body. The horse got over the dip and ran on until it was stopped by high rocks it couldn't get through. Morgan crawled up to the edge of the dip and watched the damn horse starting to run back. It stopped when it saw him and began to nibble at a clump of bunchgrass. Morgan waited for a rifle shot to kill the horse, but nothing happened. . . .

Morgan had the Winchester pushed out, moving it along the top of the line of rocks. Nothing stirred up there, and the only sound was the wind. It was so quiet down where he was that he could hear the horse tearing at the dry, rough grass. He was a target himself, no longer a good one, but still a target. Could be the shooter was running out of bullets and was waiting for him to stand up. . . .

He came out of the dip in a zig-zag run and got to the edge of the rocks without being shot. Still shook up by the hard fall, he crouched at the base of a high, flat rock, and then he moved along the rock line until he found a place where he could climb. A wide crack went up through the rocks, and he started into it. At first it was easy to climb, then the split narrowed and in one place he barely got through. For an instant he was an easy target, a sitting duck, and if the shooter had been there. . . .

He got to the top, and it opened out into a bare, wide stretch of ground with scattered rocks at the other side of it. Not a line of rocks this time, just big rocks scattered hither and yon, but good enough to make a stand in for as long as the bullets lasted. It was no more than a couple of hundred yards from where he was, but to get there he'd have to show himself and move forward with no cover. He could wait till it got dark, but by then the shooter would be gone. Morgan gave it a minute, thinking the shooter might do something. . . .

A minute got to be two, and the shooter did nothing. If the shooter was still there, he was waiting. The sun was fierce and dust blew in Morgan's face, and he had no canteen, and it would be a bitch to wait all day in the sun without water. Deciding the hell with that, he started to crawl out. . . .

A bullet chipped rock close to his head, and he rolled back into cover. There was just one shot, and the shooter didn't fire again. Morgan stayed still, and now that he wasn't moving the bullet crease in his left side began to burn. No time to look at it now, but not much blood came through his shirt, so it couldn't be too bad. Most of the blood was dry, and he felt his shirt sticking to the shallow wound. . . .

He was thinking about water when the rifle cracked one more time. No bullet came close, and he waited for the rifle to sound again. Minutes dragged by and nothing happened. All he heard was the hot wind whistling through the split in the rocks. Time stretched out, and when he looked up at the sky, there were buzzards wheeling, banking and swooping, getting ready to light down. He didn't move until the first carrion bird swept down from behind the rocks where the shooter would be. . . .

He found Heckwelder sprawled dead with the Henry rifle still gripped in his hand. The sun winked off the brass frame of the old rifle. He had put the muzzle in his mouth and pulled the trigger. The bullet was still in his head: the Henry didn't have that much velocity. Or else he had a skull like iron. . . .

It was Heckwelder all right. No mistaking the gambler's getup, the waxed mustache. Morgan found nothing on the body but a gold watch and a few dollars. Probably the watch was stolen, maybe had belonged to one of the dead stage passengers. . . .

Morgan left the body where it was and went back to bury Kate O'Hara. Without a shovel, all he could do was drag the body off the road and cover it with rocks. She had been a fiesty little woman, all right in her way. There was no sign of her pony. His own horse followed him down to the bottom of the hill and moped around until Morgan was ready to go on. . . .

Before he did he looked at the wound. Like he thought, it wasn't much, more like a burn put there by a hot poker.

God, he was tired.

Chapter Twelve

Early Saturday afternoon was a good time to get to McHargville. The town was crowded with miners and other thirsty working men looking forward to the weekly drunk. Some had gotten an early start on it, and there were drunken men in the streets, going into saloons or staggering out of them, but for most the real nighttime celebrating was still hours ahead. Already the sidewalks were splashed with beer vomit, and in one place a miner with a broken head sat in a pool of blood, talking to a deputy marshal who was telling him to get up and go home.

Morgan stabled his horse and headed for the stage office, wondering where Van Wert was, hoping to keep out of his way as long as possible. But as he knew damn well, unless Van Wert had left town or hadn't yet arrived, he was going to run into him before the week was over. Van Wert had looked for him along the road from Carson and would be looking for him still, but it seemed like he hadn't put much effort into it. If Van Wert had wanted to put a gun on him he could have waited in some place he'd had to pass.

Morgan went clear to the end of the main street to reach the stage division headquarters. Beyond it were the barns and other buildings. On the sidewalk outside the office, a whiskery man with a bulb nose was talking to a man holding a grip. Morgan went in and a woman, about forty or older, looked up from a desk and asked what she could do for him. She would have been better looking than she was if not for the thin line of her mouth, and Morgan guessed at widowhood or the man who got away. He asked for Mr. Frank Eaton, and she went to the door and called the whiskery man inside and then went back to her work at the desk in the corner.

Eaton, a short man about fifty, was as full of ginger as his whiskers. Morgan guessed he was tough enough behind the facial hair and the black suit, too heavy for Nevada heat. You didn't get to be a division superintendent by playing at businessman. "Ah yes," he said when Morgan said his name and told who he was, "I was told you'd be joining the company, but now I'm told you're not. How can I help you, Mr. Morgan?"

Before Morgan could answer Eaton went on with, "If you're here to ask me questions, well, then I can't help you at all. I think you should know that."

Morgan didn't like Eaton but kept his temper and went ahead, as if he hadn't heard. "Three men—Tobias Canty, Martin Heckwelder, Hamish Fife—can you tell me if they applied to you for jobs between six months and a year ago? Do you have records like that? Heckwelder may have used the name Buford De Forest."

Eaton held up his hand and put a pained expression on his face, what Morgan could see of it. "Didn't you hear what I just said. I am not at liberty to provide you with any information relating to this company. Take it up with Mr. Butterfield. I can tell you that I was not here during the time you mention. I have been here only three months. Mr.

Theron Vail was division superintendent before me."

"Where can I find him?"

"Mr. Vail has been dead for three months. Now, sir—"

Morgan kept at it. "I'd think you'd want to help me. These three men have been robbing your stages."

Eaton took a silver watch from his vest pocket and looked at it though there was a big clock ticking on the wall. "You're wasting my time, sir, and your own. I don't know what business U.S. Marshal Van Wert has with you, but he's been in here asking about you. If you have information about these men take it to him. He's stopping at the Scotland Hotel. Where will you be if the marshal returns?"

"I'm not at liberty to say," Morgan said, and went out. Fuck it! He'd come all the way from Carson only to run into a hardhead like Eaton, and it was hard to decide if Eaton had orders to shut him out or was doing it on his own. But Eaton knew the horse deal was off, and only Butterfield could have told him that by telegraph, so Butterfield must have given the no-talk order. Maybe not. Division superintendents were jealous of their authority, and it would be natural for Eaton to resent any outsider even if he was no longer a threat to his job. Morgan nearly smiled when he thought of breaking into the stage office in the middle of the night. What in hell would he look for in all the piles of books he'd be sure to find? It would be just his luck to be caught by some deputy checking doors after the town had gone to bed.

He was at the corner when he heard a woman calling his name, and when he turned, there was the woman from the office hurrying to catch up with him. She slowed when she knew he'd seen her and came the rest of the way in a more ladylike manner. "Mr. Morgan," she said when she got close. "I hope you won't think this forward of me but—but I couldn't help overhearing your conversation with Mr. Eaton."

"Yes, Miss," Morgan said.

She colored slightly. "It's missus. Mrs. Philpot Newbold. I'm a widow. I couldn't help—Mr. Eaton thinks I've gone out to get a soft drink, but I mustn't be too long. Those records you were asking about. We do have them, but you can't see them now. Is it true what you said about the robberies, those men?"

Morgan nodded. "It's true, Mrs. Newbold."

"Please call me Alice. Yours is Lee, isn't it?"

Morgan hoped the whiskery gent from the office wouldn't come along and fire his only source of information. "Yes, Alice," he said. "About those records—"

She didn't like to be hurried in spite of what she'd said. "I think it's very officious of Mr. Eaton not to have shown you the book. I don't know what he can be thinking, well, yes, I can. Well, I think it's my duty to help you. Can you come to my house at eleven-thirty tonight? I'll have the book."

Morgan didn't know what she was up to and he didn't care. Duty, he felt sure, wasn't part of it. "Can't it be earlier?"

"No," she said firmly. "It's Saturday night and I'm going to the tent show with Mr. Lyman from the bank. I'll be home by eleven-fifteen and ready for you by eleven-thirty, all right. No earlier please. Mr. Lyman is very jealous. Here's how to find me. . . ."

She hurried away, and Morgan crossed the street wondering what was going on. There was something cracked about the woman, but what was so different about that? It wasn't much past two o'clock and he had a lot of time to kill. Going back along the main street he passed Fallon's office. Fallon was on the second floor of a small brick building, with a painless dentist above him, a doctor below. He was a specialist in mining law and land investment, a sign said. He doubted that Fallon would be in his office so late on a Saturday afternoon. Anyway, it was better to wait and see what Mrs. Newbold's record book had to tell him. Please call me Alice, he thought sourly.

She had buried Newbold and was looking to throw a loop on this Lyman from the bank. Not fair. She was the finest woman in the world provided she brought home the bacon and didn't bring Van Wert aiong as a side order. He wondered if Eaton could have put her up to this bamboozle.

He had to duck into a bread store when he saw Van Wert coming out of a beat-up hotel on the other side of the street. Another much older badged man was trailing behind him and Van Wert was talking over his shoulder. The two men stood on the sidewalk and then Van Wert pointed for the deputy to go one way and he went the other. They were checking the hotels, what else could it be? Morgan waited till he saw the last of Van Wert's back before he came out.

It seemed safe enough to go the same way as the deputy. Van Wert knew what he looked like and the deputy didn't. A description wasn't much to go on if you didn't stand out in a crowd, didn't dress like Bill Cody or have a hump on your back. The deputy marshal was unexpected, and Morgan wondered if there was more than one. Malley said Van Wert had to be the hero of every hair-raiser he played in. Malley was what they called an honorable crook, meaning that he liked to gather his money with a net instead of a club. What Van Wert was remained to be seen.

Renting a hotel room was no good. They'd find him if they looked long enough. Coming into town he'd passed a big old house with broken windows and miners drinking beer on the sagging porch. It didn't have a sign, but it couldn't be anything but a boardinghouse. It had to be Irish or Cornish, not both—the lads from Ireland and Cornwall were always fighting. It had the look of bedbugs, but that didn't matter a damn. Question was, would they rent him a room?

Morgan got down from his horse, and the men on the porch busied themselves with their bottles and beer pails. No one looked at him—maybe they thought he was some kind of law. They were a wild looking bunch all right, distant and hostile, but clean enough for men who worked underground, making money for fat men in San Francisco.

"I'm looking for a room," Morgan said to one stocky man who looked less hostile than the others. "One or two nights, is all."

The man took a clay pipe from his mouth, knocked the bowl on the heel of his boot, then yelled through the open door, "Cafferty, there's a man out here says he's needin' a room."

Cafferty came out, a big man about forty with one arm. He didn't sound as Irish as the man with the clay pipe. "I think somebody's try to play a joke on you. We don't put up nobody here but miners, and a lovely lot they are, as you can see."

"I'd be obliged," Morgan said. "I won't get in the way."

Cafferty allowed himself a smile. "That would be advisable, yes, it would." Some of the miners laughed. "Well all right, a dollar a night is what I charge. For that you get a bed and a chair and a lovely calendar for the year before last." That got another laugh, a little better natured this time. "You can wash up out back."

Morgan paid for one night and got a room on the second floor. There was no key to the door, but Cafferty said nobody would dare steal a man's goods in his place. "I would break their back," he said. Morgan didn't doubt him for a minute. He stretched out on the bed and slept for a while.

Later, still on the bed, he listened to the sounds downstairs. It was after nine and Saturday night at Cafferty's was going full swing. Somebody was beating on a piano that didn't have all the notes, and they were singing Irish songs. So far there were no fights, but that would come, and one-armed Cafferty had to be pretty good to keep this bunch in line. But for all the noise they made nobody came to his door, nobody bothered him. At eleven o'clock he started for Mrs. Newbold's.

It was a small two-story house with a garden and a peeling white fence. The street was quiet, no saloons, no eating places, and Mr. Newbold must have had a few bucks to live there. Lights were in the downstairs windows, and there was no sign of Mr. Lyman from the bank. The door opened before he had gotten to it, but she covered her eagerness by saying, "That garden gate squeaks so, I must remember to have it oiled."

Morgan hadn't heard any gate. "Eleven-thirty," he said.

She showed him into the main room, a space too small for all the furniture in it. There were glass-fronted book-cases and pictures everywhere, all neat and shining and hung straight. A bottle of sherry and two glasses stood on a table at the end of a sofa. The small fire in a big fireplace wasn't doing much to ward off the cold of a Nevada night. There was no sign of a records book.

"I'm afraid all I can offer you is sherry," she said after Morgan sat down. "It's from California but not at all bad. Why don't you try it and decide for yourself."

Morgan didn't know what it tasted like except sweet. It could have been hair tonic for all he knew. "Very tasty," he said.

"Mr. Forbes Ferguson was very funny as Algernon," she said. "A very funny play, The Counterfeit Duke. You should have heard Mr. Lyman laugh."

Morgan thought he could live his life without that. How could he tell her to get on with it without getting her back up. She was a prickly woman and sounded like she'd been having more than a few sips of this California embroca-tion. She was easy on the eye, even with the turned down mouth that spoke of bitterness and disappointment, and if she'd only let up on the lady-lady bullshit that wasn't real anyway, he knew he'd like her a lot better. He didn't want to hear any more about Algernon, but he didn't want to be turned out for being a boor.

She had another drink—he wasn't supposed to notice—and then sat down heavily beside him. "I want to help you because I feel I must, no matter what Mr. Eaton says, these terrible robberies, he should—but you see Mr. Eaton is worried about his job, all those children. Are you married by the way?"

"For ten years," Morgan said before he changed course and added, "but we live apart now. You know how it is."

"Indeed I don't," she said laughing. "Mr. Newbold and I were very happy together. But I feel for you," and saying that she felt his thigh and he felt his cock stiffen. Then reaching for another drink she added, "I'm a Moorhead of an old New Hampshire family and I find myself working in a stagecoach office." She laughed like vinegar. "I suppose I should show you that book. That's all you came for, isn't it?"

Gallantly Morgan said, "Some of that is true, but not all of it. I'm pleased to know you, Alice." Morgan playing Algernon, who would have said it better.

"Liar!" she said. "But women like to be lied to, as no doubt you know. Now I'd better show you the book before you get too romantic, you wicked man."

Morgan had been called many things in his time, but never wicked or romantic. She took the book from under the sofa and got another drink while he was paging through it. He found Canty and Fife and Heckwelder and the reasons why they had been turned down for jobs. "Shiftless looking," for Canty. "Not suited, unreliable," for Heckwelder. "Habitual drunkard," for Fife. Theron Vail might be dead, but he'd been a good judge of men. With these three ginks he was right on target. All the dates before the names were before the robberies.

"I found three of the names I wanted," he said. "What is this book? A black list?"

"That's right. All the division superintendents have a book like that. A monthly list is sent to Carson City and a general list is sent out from there. It helps to keep undesirables from getting work in other divisions. But it's not foolproof. Some of them give different names and are hired anyway. Is something bothering you?" She moved closer as she said that.

Morgan knew better than to move away from her wine breath. "There's a fourth man, but I don't know his name." He told her the dates in the book. "Were you working there then?"

"Well, yes." She moved closer. "But I can't say I remember those men or their names. Men are in and out all the time. Mr. Vail talked to them when I started eight months ago after Mr. Newbold died and I was forced to take employment. This fourth man, can you describe him?"

"That's the trouble. The way I was told he looks, he could be a hundred men. Thirty to thirty-five. Five ten. Brown hair. Round face. Not good looking, not bad looking. Sometimes wears a mustache. Average in every way, the man said."

Beside him Morgan felt Mrs. Newbold shaking with laughter. "Dave Fanshaw would hate to be called average," she said. Her face had the look of someone about to play a trump card. "Dave Fanshaw, it has to be Dave. The mustache, he kept growing it and shaving it off, as if he couldn't make up his mind how he wanted to look. The last time I saw him he was clean shaven, the conceited son of a bitch."

"He's here in town?"

"Oh, yes." Her smile would have soured molasses. "He's here, but you won't find him in that book. He had my job for a short while. He stayed for a few days to show me how the books were kept. A real charmer, he thinks he is. Now he works for a lawyer named Fallon."

There it was, Morgan thought. It was beginning to fit, but there were pieces missing. He didn't have to guess what Fanshaw had done to her. Led her down the primrose path and left her there. Now she had a chance to pay him back.

"I don't know what he does for Fallon," she said without being asked. "Fallon has an office in town, but he lives on a ranch some miles out, I'm not sure how far, a big place from what I hear. A gentleman farmer or rancher he thinks he is, but he's certainly no gentleman. They say he's a crook, some scandal back East before he came here, it was in the paper."

Morgan took her hand when she reached for his. She wanted to talk so he said nothing. "Sometimes I see him going into the office, Dave, I mean. I always thought he was too bright to be working at what I do now. But it's all right for a woman, isn't it? Like hell it is, I hate it. Does all this help you, Lee?"

"Helps a lot," Morgan said. "You don't talk to him anymore, is that right? I don't mean to pry."

That made her laugh. "Of course you mean to pry, that's why you're here. It's all right though. Yes, Dave and I were quite close at one time. At first I was amused by his conceit, such a brash young man, not that's he's so much younger than I am. He just seems younger than he is. Dave has such a high opinion of himself it used to make me laugh and sometimes it made him angry. And yet here he is working for a crook like Fallon. Oh there's a lot I could tell you about Dave, about a lot of things."

"I wish you would," Morgan said, not sure she had that much more to tell. But there was nothing to be lost by listening. So close now, he was willing to listen to her till she got lockjaw, and even if booze made her jump the rails and start on the late Mr. Newbold or some such bullshit, he'd try to get her back on track. If Fanshaw and Fallon hadn't run out by now they'd still be around in the morning.

After another drink she stretched out on the sofa with her head on his lap. Her upswept hair had come undone and he ran his fingers through it and she sighed. The kind of woman she was, there was no use trying to prompt her. He'd seen the fierce anger in her eyes when she started to put the knife to Fanshaw. Any wrong move he made—

that and the booze—could turn her into a screaming wild-cat. The cold ones were often like that.

"Lee," she said after a while, "there's something I must tell you."

"Yes, Alice." Morgan went on playing with her hair.

She sniffed and gave a little laugh. "Lee, you need a bath. Please, don't be offended, but it's true. You've been on the road for days. Why don't you let me give you a bath? Don't be shocked. I used to give Mr. Newbold baths all the time. Imagine that—a minister! Yes, that's what he was, but he liked the earthly pleasures. Why not? We were married, after all."

Holy Christ! Morgan thought, he was going to get a bath from a dead minister's wife. Well he could grab his hat and run out of there, but what would that get him? It wouldn't get him a bath, and it sure as hell wouldn't get him any more information.

"Come on," she said, getting up and pulling him to his feet. "I like doing things for nice men. Mr. Newbold was a nice man and so are you. Mr. Newbold was a man of moderate means, but he insisted on the luxury of a bathtub. There are not many bathtubs in McHargville."

Morgan wondered if she had given Fanshaw any baths. Probably had soaped him up good. He allowed himself to be led upstairs to a small bathroom on the second floor. The tub was small and behind it was a big copper hot-water tank on a sturdy support. She laughed when she saw him looking at the tank.

"Don't worry, you're not going to get a cold bath. Hot water comes from the kitchen stove and it's all ready. Let me help you get out of your clothes." She unbuttoned his pants and took his cock out. "Oh my, will you look at that! You're as ready as the hot water."

She dragged down his pants while the tub was filling. At first there was so much steam it was hard to see, and by the time it cleared she had all his clothes off and most of hers. She threw off what was left and pushed him down into the hot water and, by God, it felt good after the cold downstairs. "I'm going to scrub you till you shine," she said. Morgan thought he heard Rev. Newbold turning over in his grave.

The long-handled back brush she used on him was just what he needed for his sore muscles. She lathered up lemon soap until the whole bathroom smelled of it. Then she climbed into the tub and sat facing him and told him to scrub her. It was a tight fit in the tub and they had to turn this way and that to get comfortable. Laughing gaily, she tossed the brush away, grabbed his cock and put his middle finger in her cunt, and while he diddled her she soaped his cock and stroked it so fast he thought he was going to shoot his wad right there in the tub. She came after a few strokes of his fingers, and that was fine for her, but not for him. He didn't want to shoot his into a fistful of soap, he wanted to get into her, to move her so she'd hang over the sloping end of the tub and he could get into her from behind. It took some shifting to arrange that, and she kept laughing while he moved her. At last she was in position with her legs spread, and he rose up behind her and shoved it all the way in. There was a scream and she kicked her legs, splashing water all over the floor, and she kept on kicking and jerking while he shafted her like a machine. It must have hurt to be fucked like that, with her head and shoulders hanging out of the tub, but it didn't stop her from laughing. The only time she stopped was when she climaxed, and screamed, and there wasn't much difference between the two sounds. Now that she'd let herself go she was a wild woman and a fine fuck, and he knew how wrong he was when he thought her a cold bitch with a steel trap for a cunt.

But for all their exertions they started to get cold. The water was getting a chill to it and the wet white walls looked cold. It was well after midnight and the hardest part of the Nevada night was setting in. He'd already come once and now he quickened his stroke and came again. Once they were out of the tub there might not be another chance. The booze had to be dying in her, and she might turn back into a proper lady. He hoped that wouldn't happen, but he had no complaints, no matter how it turned out.

She did stop laughing but that was all. "No, no," she said when he made a show of reaching for his pants. "Never mind the towel. We'll dry off in bed and snuggle up close and get warm. I'll rub your back, all those bruises, such a burn, never mind, don't tell me where you got them."

In bed they got dry and warm, and she rubbed his back until he felt sleepy. Kate O'Hara had seen the bruises, but hadn't rubbed anything except his cock. Poor old Kate. He'd run into a lot of interesting women lately. First Margaret Deakin and now this one, Mrs. Newbold—Alice—who had been a revelation. He hoped Lyman at the bank was worthy of her, that is, if she managed to snare him. Snare him! The fucker should be glad to get her.

They slept for a few hours and he was awake before she was. Finally she woke and they fucked till dawn, and then she made coffee and bacon and eggs and told him gently that it was time to go before the neighbors were up and about. He didn't think there was anything more to learn about Fanshaw and Fallon, and he didn't ask.

She said it herself before she opened the door. "I kept you here by false pretenses. I hope you don't mind."

"Lord, no," he said, putting on his hat. "I wanted to stay."

"Lee." She clutched at his arm. "Last night was wonderful, but it has to be our last and only night. Don't come back and spoil things, will you. Mr. Lyman and I are to be married next month. Mr. Lyman is a very nice man, a widower—and he's sixty-five."

Morgan kissed her and opened the door. "Put him in the bathtub, Alice."

He heard her laughing as he went away.

Chapter Thirteen

Morgan walked back to Cafferty's through the Sunday-morning town, and it was quiet except for the dull thump of the crushers up at the mine that never stopped, night or day. Steam and the smell of hot engines drifted down from the long hill where the mine was, and the sun wasn't warm yet, and he thought of the bed he'd just left and wished he could be back there. The saloons were closed and no drunks were asleep in the streets. It looked like this thing was coming close to the end, but he felt a bit forlorn. Look on the bright side, he thought, nobody could say he wasn't clean, and he smiled at the thought.

He would need the binoculars to look at Fallon's place. Going out there without them would be no good. Going in blind could get him shot, and he had been through too much to let that happen. A cracked bell was clacking in some church tower and he thought Sunday was a good day to be going out to Fallon's. At least he wouldn't be in his office on Sunday, or wasn't likely to be. Alice said he lived out on the North Road. He would ask Cafferty.

Cafferty was drunk on the porch when he got back to the boardinghouse. Morgan didn't know where he'd got the idea that Cafferty didn't drink. Didn't drink because he had to deal with too many drunks. Maybe he'd heard him say it and hadn't paid too much attention. But he was drunk now.

He lurched up from the battered rocker when Morgan came close. He was good and drunk, and it looked like he'd been waiting. His empty shirt sleeve had come unpinned, and it flapped in the warming-up wind. "Just the man I want to see," he said, coming down the steps.

"Morning, Mr. Cafferty," Morgan said.

Cafferty cocked his head to one side. "You could be an Idaho man by the sound of you, am I right or am I wrong?"

"That's where I'm from." Morgan wondered what was going on, why he'd asked. "You ever been there?"

Cafferty laughed like a lunatic. "Have I ever been there?" His laugh got louder. "Well, of course, sure I've been there, and I left my arm behind so they wouldn't forget me." Cafferty grabbed his empty sleeve and shook it. "A deputy sheriff company lickspittle hired scab thug took off this wing with a shotgun. A mine strike in the Coeur d'Alene, and they would have used Maxim guns if they'd had them. They hunted me through the woods because I was an organizer. I'd have bled to death if a farm family hadn't taken me in, hidden me, and patched me up the best they could. I've had two operations since then."

Morgan didn't know what to say. Cafferty blocked his way when he tried to get past. "You never were a deputy, were you, nothing like that?"

"I raise horses," Morgan said. "Always have." Cafferty let him pass, and he started for the stairs. A hard luck story was the last thing he wanted to hear. Cafferty had seemed so sound, what the hell was eating him? He opened the door to his room and knew the reason. Van Wert was standing to one side of the window, pointing a cocked gun at him. Morgan heard a sound behind him, but didn't turn. A hand took his gun.

"Walk in, and put your hands behind you," Van Wert said.

Handcuffs snapped around Morgan's wrists, and the door closed. The door creaked as the deputy leaned against it. "Stretch out on the bed," Van Wert said. "You've been dodging and ducking, but this is where it ends. This is the last time you'll get in my way."

Morgan had to lie on his side because of the handcuffs. The man at the door—not too tall, powerfully built—looked at him with a faint grin. He was the same man who'd been checking the hotels, a mean bastard by the look of him.

"Am I going to jail, or what?" Morgan said.

"You're staying here with Coffey," Van Wert said. "You're safer here than in some town jail. You might just walk out when they let the Saturday drunks loose. Dumber things have happened in town jails." Coffey smiled, but Van Wert didn't. "Later—when I get back—we'll see about putting you in a real jail. I warned you not to interfere—go back to Idaho, I said—and yet I find you here in McHarville, why is that?"

"I'm on my way home," Morgan said. "Coffey here can put me on the stage."

Coffey heaved himself away from the door. "I'd like to put you someplace."

"Quit it." Van Wert's voice was sharp. "You guard this man, that's all. If he tries to attack you—shoot him. Don't wrestle with him—shoot him. Get that?"

Coffey smiled. "Yes, sir—I'll shot him dead. How long'll you be gone, Mr. Van Wert. Those Micks downstairs—"

Van Wert didn't like that. "You'll stay till I tell you to leave. The Micks won't try anything, I warned the cripple about that. Take some good advice, Morgan—get some sleep."

Van Wert was at the door when Morgan said, "You talked to Fallon yet?"

Van Wert didn't turn to ask who Fallon was, but he hesitated before he went out, and maybe he closed the door too hard. Morgan heard him going down the bare board stairs and wondered how the hell he was going to get out of this. Coffey sat in the chair and waited for Van Wert to get clear of the house before he started talking. He didn't like Van Wert, Morgan thought, but he was afraid of him, a sensible attitude for any man who wasn't a fool.

But Coffey was a fool, brutal and crafty, but still a fool. "You're lucky you're dealin' with Mr. Van Wert 'stead of me. Left to me I would put you on crutches in the old soldiers' home."

Morgan didn't tell him to go fuck himself. U.S. Deputy Marshal Coffey might get carried away. "Mr. Van Wert wouldn't like that."

Coffey hunched his muscle-banded shoulders, trying to get more comfortable on the hard chair. "I could say you tried to get my gun and I had to beat you over the head."

"You're not supposed to get that close," Morgan said. "You're to shoot me dead if I try anything." If he had his hands free there might be a chance. In handcuffs he was dead meat.

"I wouldn't mind killin' you," Coffey said, thinking it over. "Don't be givin' me ideas, if you know what I mean. I don't like people from Idaho."

Morgan asked how that came to be, and it turned out that Coffey meant Ohio. His wife was from Ohio, and was a bitch. It was not the most interesting conversation of Morgan's life, but he knew he'd remember it. As long as Coffey stayed in his chair, kept on talking, the threat of mayhem stayed bottled up. But it always came back to violence, what Coffey would like to do to him, to other people.

It was as plain as Coffey's big nose that he wanted to kill somebody. Nobody special, just somebody, and Morgan wondered why Van Wert would want such a murderous savage underfoot. To do his dirty work—why else? Coffey would do anything he was told to do, and Van Wert would cover for him and keep him on the payroll.

Now Coffey was asking where Idaho was, and Morgan was telling him. Coffey was saying Idaho must be a real shitass place if it wasn't a state yet. The morning dragged on like that, and it got to be afternoon. It got later than that, and Coffey was telling Morgan how he'd like to drown him in a cesspool. There was a rap on the door.

Coffey stayed on the chair. "Fuck off," he said when there was another knock. At the third knock he got up cursing, and when he opened the door there was nobody there. A fourth knock sent him bounding out of the chair, and he jerked the door open and stuck his head out yelling. Something hit him and he dropped like a stone.

Cafferty looked in with a wink saying, "That's how you do it, make them mad enough to get careless, then bam!" Cafferty was drunk, but steady. He dragged Coffey inside and got the handcuffs key from his pocket and let Morgan loose. "Threatened me, a man like me, called me a cripple, the Dutch bastard." Cafferty was mad. Morgan was glad to see him.

"You'll get into trouble for this," Morgan said, getting off the bed.

Cafferty was putting the handcuffs on Coffey. "I been in trouble before. Did he see me? He did not. I got a hundred Irishmen to swear I never laid a glove on him, and I can get more."

Morgan got his gun and put it in its holster. "Can you keep the deputy here, I don't know for how long?"

"Long as you like. You want the deputy in a crusher I can arrange that, the boys below. The Dutchman can go in after him if you like, the both of them, the night shift, dust to dust—but quicker."

Morgan put on his hat. "Not yet. Thanks, Cafferty."

"For nothing," Cafferty said. "I owe some good Idaho people—and I hate the police."

The stableman told him how to get to Fallon's ranch. About seven miles out, a big sign, no way to miss it, and Fallon's road was better than the country. It was evening now and getting dark, and the town was quiet; the saloons were open and the stores were closed, no drunks in the street. People were coming out of a church after some late doings. A town deputy talking to one of the church people gave Morgan no more than a glance as he rode by.

Van Wert had been gone since morning, and Morgan wondered what he'd been doing all that time. An easy ride out and back wouldn't take more than a couple of hours, if that, so there was a lot of time to be accounted for. No use trying to figure it, Van Wert could be anywhere. Morgan didn't want to meet him on the road and listened for a horse coming the other way. But there was nothing, not even a wagon, and the dark road was deserted all the way out.

Even in the dark he could see the high white gate from a long way off. It looked to be just a gate, with no wire running away from either side of it. He didn't know why he had the idea that Fallon's property would be fenced. The binoculars didn't help much because there wasn't enough light. He got down and led his horse along the side of the road, where it was mostly sand. He reached the gate without being challenged. No one was there. Two tall white-painted wood columns supported a sign with the name Fallon in foot-high black letters on a white background. It was the kind of thing only a braggart would put up.

He couldn't see a house from where he was, no lights at all, and the road went away into low dark hills. No plan came to mind because he didn't know what he'd find in there. There could be a fence and guards closer to the house. It didn't make sense for Fallon not to have men watching for him, knowing that he'd killed Canty and was after the rest of them.

Coming out of the hills, about a mile from the gate, he saw the fence and the swing gate the road went through, and if there were guards, that's where they'd be. A match flared and went out. Someone was there all right, at least one man was. He listened for the sound of men talking, but the wind was blowing the other way. The light came and went as clouds ran across the face of the moon. Mostly it was dark, and he could see the glow of the cigarette every time the smoker drew on it. He tied the horse to a bush and hoped it would hold. After that he went ahead on foot, moving out wide until he came to the fence, four strands of barbed wire with posts.

Crawling under the bottom wire was easy enough—only a few rips in his shirt. After he got through, the moon cleared and he lay flat until it was dark enough to start back along the fence. The cigarette no longer burned, and all he could see was the side of the gate. Then another match flared, and he was able to make out a man standing behind the gate, cupping his hands around a cigarette. The guard was smoking, shifting from one foot to the other, when Morgan rose up behind him and laid his gun barrel along the side of his neck. Morgan hit him again while he was falling, then tied him securely with long strips cut from his canvas coat and gagged him with his bandanna. Unless he was a bull of a man he'd be out for hours.

Morgan took the guard's rifle and pistol—never leave weapons behind unless you have to—and put them in a clump of brush after he started down the road. The road went over a low hill and when he got to the top he saw the house a good way off, with plenty of light showing. The house was long and low, solid looking like a hacienda, and the outbuildings and a huge barn stood at some remove from it; valley land stretched away behind it for miles. Too far out for him to see clearly was the movement of cattle. Fallon was doing pretty well for himself. There was even a windbreak, not anywhere near its full growth, but a sign that Fallon meant to stay.

Morgan stayed on the road for a while, stopping now and then to listen. All he heard was the faint creak of a windmill, the movement of the blades turning. He got close enough to see better. There was no bunkhouse, nothing that shape, so Fallon probably kept no more than a few Herefords. Still there had to be some men on the place.

He was off the road and moving through the windbreak when a man who was hunkered down by a tree grabbed his rifle and tried to get up. Morgan kicked him in the face and the back of his head hit the tree and he slid down and lay still. Morgan tied and gagged him, listening for sounds. Two men down, he thought. Two men could do the work on a place like this, but there could be more, and he moved cautiously to the edge of the trees.

Now he was close enough to hear men talking inside an open window—not a French window—tall and high and it started about a foot from the ground. He didn't know what Fallon or Fanshaw sounded like, but he thought he recognized Van Wert's drawling voice. The tall window threw light a long way out, and he kept away from it. It opened in like a door and when he edged close to it, he heard Van Wert talking and then another man cutting in to say something.

Van Wert said, "It's not as simple as you think."

The other man said, "You just leave that to me, my boy."

Morgan took off his hat and looked around the edge of the window. The window was narrow, and he couldn't see the entire room. Van Wert was standing to one side of a blazing fire. A thick man in his fifties was behind a desk. Another man, thirty or so, sat on a studded leather sofa. Fanshaw. He was the right age, had brown hair, a round face. He had a glass in his hand and was smirking to himself. The man at the desk—Fallon—looked and sounded slightly drunk. A bottle and glass were beside him.

Morgan gave it a minute. Fallon was calling Van Wert my boy again. Well now, Morgan thought, what have we here? "We mustn't bring Butterfield too deeply into this," Fallon said to Van Wert. "It was a business arrangement, and he doesn't want to know too much about it."

Fanshaw said, "Butterfield is up to his balls in it."

"Yes, Dave," Fallon said mildly, reaching for the bottle. "Thanks to you he is, and so am I if it comes to that. But there's nothing here Van can't make right, isn't that so, Van, my boy?"

"Van can make anything right," Fanshaw said, the smirk pasted to his face.

Van Wert stood straighter. "*Mister* Van Wert to you."

Fallon rapped for order with the bottom of the bottle, like a judge. "Enough of that, we're all friends here." He pointed the neck of the bottle of Fanshaw. "You take too much on yourself, that's your trouble. You say they got drunk and you couldn't control them. I don't believe you. You fed them the whiskey, egged them on, is what you did. You had strict orders, never, never kill anybody, don't bother the women—*never!* Why did you do it?"

Fanshaw drank some of his drink. "Butterfield can't back out now."

Fallon's sudden anger came and went. "Ah, Dave, there was no need for it. You heard Van was coming to take over and you thought that would be the end of it. You thought there'd be no more need for you. You thought we'd drop the plan because of Van and you wouldn't come in for the money. So you did something terrible."

Fanshaw looked at Van Wert. "You should have told me Mr. Van Wert was in with you."

Fallon spread his hands like an advocate appealing to a jury. "You can't expect to be told everything, Dave. That's not the way of business."

Van Wert said, "Look here. We have to come to some decision or I'm leaving."

Fanshaw was looking at Fallon. "I thought it wasn't just business with us."

Fallon said, "You would have been told, don't I always, when the time was ripe."

Van Wert moved away from the fireplace. "This whole thing is ripe. I'll be back tomorrow when I can maybe get a straight answer."

Morgan stepped over the windowsill with his gun in his hand and didn't see the man in the chair in the corner until his hand moved toward his gun. "Don't do it," Morgan said. "Don't touch it, sit on your hands." The man was young, maybe a gunman, but didn't look too eager to die.

Morgan swung his gun back to cover the others. He knew Van Wert could have shot him, but hadn't made a move. Maybe he didn't think he was fast enough. Fanshaw was staring at Morgan. Fallon was saying for Christ's sake what's going on here, for Christ's sake no shooting. "No shooting," he said to the man sitting on his hands.

"I thought you had this man locked up," he said to Van Wert.

Fallon had hair like a washboard going back from a long widow's peak. A slack mouth gave him the look of a carnival barker. "You're not supposed to be here," he said to Morgan, "but since you are why don't you put away that gun and listen to the reality of it?"

Morgan stayed as he was. It was four against one here, but he had to think about Van Wert and the gunman. Fanshaw didn't have a gun that showed and neither did Fallon. Just the same.

Van Wert hadn't said anything. Now he said, "Give me the gun, Morgan. I'm a United States marshal here on official business. You're making this worse for yourself." He held out his hand.

"Keep your hands still." Morgan moved the gun so it was pointing at Van Wert.

Fallon laughed. "Too late for badge talk, Van, he knows. Now looka here, Mr. Morgan—"

Morgan kept the gun on Van Wert. Shit! Four men he might have to shoot at, but he was still betting on Van Wert and the gunman. It had to come to killing, in the end. He couldn't walk out, and they couldn't let him.

Fallon cut into his thoughts by saying, "There's no need for all this, Mr. Morgan. I know why you're here and it's all been a terrible and tragic mistake. It wasn't meant to happen the way it did."

Fallon was warming up for a jury of one. Morgan wanted to kill him where he sat. "You think you can explain it away, what they did, you did?"

Fallon sat up straight. "I didn't tell them to do what they did. It was meant as business pressure, that's all, like putting vinegar in a competitor's milk pails. Disrupt the stage business a bit, then buy it cheap. No killing or getting rough with the passengers, no bothering the women."

"But a woman is dead because of you," Morgan said quietly, thinking he could kill Fallon before the others killed him. Fallon looked like an able, intelligent man, and Morgan wondered why he had to bother with crookedness. Maybe he liked the risk more than the money. Some men were like that.

"I am very sorry for that," Fallon said. "That was a bad thing you did, Dave. Anyone else but you I'd turn over to the law."

Fanshaw gave a defiant laugh. "But you can do that, can you?"

Fallon stared at him, but said nothing.

Morgan thought he should put them together, where he could watch them better. No good, too much movement. But he had to do something pretty soon. Maybe he should try for Van Wert and the gunman, then turn his gun on the other two. It couldn't drag on like this. Nobody was coming to help him.

"Mr. Morgan," Fallon said. "You mind if I have a drink? I promise not to throw the bottle at you."

"Better not." Morgan knew he was stalling as much as Fallon. Stalling for what? Nothing was going to change.

Fallon was careful the way he poured the drink. Fanshaw's glass was on the floor, and he was reaching to pick it up. "Leave it. Stay still," Fallon said hastily. "You can have one later."

"I want a drink now." Fanshaw put on a face like a spoiled child.

Fallon drank and smacked his loose lips. Old or not he was a bold bastard, Morgan thought. "Now listen here, Mr. Morgan," he said, getting more boldness from the whiskey. "What we have here is a standoff, a deadlock. You have us at gunpoint, yet what can you do? March us off at gunpoint, lock us up in the town jail. And even if the marshal believed you, which is very doubtful, what then? But none of that is going to happen, is it?"

Van Wert hadn't said anything for a while. Fanshaw was staring at Fallon. The gunman didn't move in his chair.

"There are too many of us," Fallon said, going on with his argument. "You can't be that good with a gun, you can't kill all of us without getting shot. I have a gun right here in my drawer. You want to take it?"

"Leave it," Morgan said.

"Well there you are," Fallon said. "You don't want anything to tip the balance, isn't that right? But I know what you're thinking, and you're right. This must be brought to some conclusion, an amicable conclusion, agreeable to all, I hope. Let us reason together, sir."

Morgan looked at him.

"Silence gives consent, I hope," Fallon said after a sip of whiskey. "What started all this was a simple idea for taking the ownership of the Nevada Stage Lines from Mr.

John Butterfield's rheumatic hands. William Butterfield, the bastard son, hates his father and wished to be free of him. I suggested how it could be done, and he agreed. But no killing. Willy is a weak man, but has a good heart. I agreed. Of course, no killing. It was working well, and then Mr. Fanshaw had to go and spoil it."

Fanshaw jumped from the sofa. "Fuck you, Charles. "I'll tear your scraggly fucking hair out!"

Chapter Fourteen

"If there are any more outbursts . . ." Fallon said after Morgan settled Fanshaw down.

The whiskey or the recklessness made Fallon laugh. "So I left the hiring of the make-believe bandits to Dave. It should have been easy enough. The state is full of petty criminals. Leave it to me, Dave said, I'll find the right men and not men with prison records, not men like that, not criminals at all, you don't want men like that, real bad men you can't control."

Fallon stared at Fanshaw. "You were afraid of real bad men, Dave. Always too clever, that's your trouble, but, you know, the men you hired, it was not their fault, and I ask you again—why did you do it?"

Fanshaw said irritably, "You've been going on about that all day. It's over and done."

Morgan wondered what Van Wert thought of all this. His face was set in grim lines, no way to tell.

Fallon poured another drink without asking if he could. "Mr. Morgan," he said, back to his courtroom manner.

"I don't know how you are financially, but I can make you a rich man. What's done is done, as Mr. Fanshaw puts it so cavalierly. Still, it's a fact. Put your righteous anger aside and come in with us. Once the stage line is in our hands you can have a contract to supply horses for the entire operation. No competition, no other bidders to worry about, you'd be set for life. Now you argue that stagecoaching is a dying business, and that's perfectly true. It is. But when the need for railroads arises they will be our railroads and they will be built where the stages run now. Already I have been buying key sections of land."

Fanshaw was muttering. Finally he burst out with, "You never told me that."

Fallon grabbed the bottle and Morgan told him to put it down. "Then you tell him to shut the fuck up," Fallon said.

Fanshaw glared at him. "You shut up, old man. You're getting nowhere."

Van Wert told Fanshaw to be quiet.

"You say that because you don't know human nature." Fallon spoke to Fanshaw without looking at him. "Mr. Morgan, no matter what we say we all like money, some of us more than others. Wouldn't you like to make a real success of your life, get out from under these penny pinching bankers up in Idaho? Of course you would. And if you have any doubts about how much money you can make, let me tell you a secret. The price of silver is going to drop, not because of market conditions, nothing like that—the government is going to force it down, no matter what Mr. Bryan says. Gold, sir—the value of gold must be maintained."

Morgan thought he heard a sound outside the window. Then some night-prowling animal sniffed around and went away.

"That's just my cat," Fallon said. "Dave hates my cat, don't you, Dave? The silver mines have to give out sometime," he said to Morgan, and then Nevada will have to turn to more stable enterprises. Ranching, farming—they're growing melons in the Washoe Valley—lumber in the mountains. Land will be cheap. You'll be able to buy whole towns cheap."

Fallon pointed to a brown bank envelope on the desk. "There's a thousand dollars in there, Mr. Morgan, and it's all yours, as a gesture of good faith. More where that came from, right here in this desk. Take it, man, it's only a start."

Morgan held the gun on Fallon while he slid the envelope into his pocket. Then he moved back to where he had been. There might be a way out of this or at least a way to buy time. It depended on how easily Fallon thought he could be bought. A crook might think that of any man. He knew damn well that Fallon had no intention of cutting him in. He was just trying to talk himself into a safer position, out of the way when the bullets started to fly.

Fallon gestured toward the gun and got an impatient look on his face. "Ah, there's no need of that, not now. You're thinking the minute I make a deal with this man Fallon he'll turn on me, shoot me in the back or have it done. And you'd be right if you were dealing with some desperado. But I'm a lawyer, not some badman who thinks the way to settle everything is with a gun. In the legal profession you must learn to compromise, and that's what I'm doing with you. I don't want to think there's a whole clan of Idaho Morgans that'll come after me seeking revenge. In short, sir, there's money enough for everyone, or there will be. Fairer than that I can't be."

"You better listen to him," Van Wert said.

"Why should I trust you, any of you?" Morgan knew he had to decide pretty soon. Pretend to let down his guard or try to get out of there some other way? He didn't think it was going to make much difference.

"I just told you why," Fallon said. "But now it's time to point something else out to you. Jimmy could have shot you when you came through that window. You're very quick with a gun, aren't you, Jimmy?"

"Very quick," the gunman said, not moving at all.

"You know why Jimmy didn't shoot you? Because he knew you could have shot me from outside the window. Jimmy doesn't fire his gun unless I tell him to."

"Don't tell him."

"Mr. Morgan," Fallon said with some exasperation, "this can't go on all night. Make up your mind: are you in or out?"

It was getting close. "What guarantee do I have that—"

"Dave here . . ." Fallon started to say. Fanshaw jumped up yelling, and the gunman pulled his gun at the same time. Morgan shot him before he knocked over the chair and fired from behind it. Morgan shot him in the head when he tried to fire again, then he swung his gun at Van Wert. Fallon was trying to get the gun from the drawer, and Fanshaw was all over him. Van Wert fired at Fallon and dropped Fanshaw instead. Fallon was raising the gun when Van Wert shot him in the shoulder, and he lurched back into his chair and dropped the gun. Van Wert picked up Fallon's gun and turned toward Morgan, his own gun still in his hand.

They faced each other. Morgan's gun was steady in his hand, still cocked. Then Van Wert holstered his gun and stuck Fallon's gun in the waistband of his pants. Fallon was mumbling in the chair, asking for a drink. Then he said, "Dave . . . what happened to Dave?"

"He's dead," Van Wert said. "So is the other one. There's just you, Fallon."

Morgan holstered his gun, still watching Van Wert. Everything had happened so fast. You knew it was coming—built up to it—and then you were surprised.

"Dave," Fallon said.

Van Wert was feeling Fallon's shoulder through his coat. "I told you he's dead. You're not shot that bad, likely the muscle. I'll fix you up."

Fallon's rubbery face was a bad color, his forehead wrinkled with puzzlement. "Why did you do it, Van? Shoot me—why? You could have killed him . . . that would be the end of it."

Morgan was thinking the same thing—why?

Fallon shouted at Morgan, "You rotten son of a bitch, you caused this whole thing! What's the matter with you? You meet some cunt on a stagecoach and she gets the pork and you go off on a crusade . . ."

Van Wert pushed him back into the chair and told him to shut up.

Fallon looked down at Fanshaw's body, then at Van Wert, then at Morgan. "He's no match for you, Van. Kill the fucker and we'll make a whole new deal, anything you say, anything you want."

Van Wert looked at Morgan. "No deal. I'm a United States marshal—"

Fallon laughed and that made him grimace with pain. "Listen you! You're as crooked as a ram's horn."

Maybe that was just the wrong thing to say. Morgan couldn't decide then, or later. He could never make up his mind about Van Wert. Usually—when he came close to it—it was always on the side of the argument that Van Wert had been in with Fallon since the beginning, but had changed his mind at the last moment. But the why always remained.

"Look," Fallon said. "I'll pass out cold if you don't give me a drink. I need a drink; I need a doctor."

Van Wert poured whiskey and held it to Fallon's mouth. "You'll get a doctor after you write a confession and sign it."

Fallon had some more whiskey in him. "Oh, for Christ's sake, Van. What is all this about? What is it you want? Everything I own? All right, you can have it, damn you. Everything I've worked for, yes. I'll sign everything over to you. I'm a lawyer. It'll be legal." Fallon was babbling, close to it. It came to him like a blow, that this time he couldn't talk his way out of trouble. Then he put on a better face and tried to calm himself.

"It's not like I'll come back to contest it. How could I? Let me take some money, and let me go. After I'm gone you can take care of this—" He waved his good arm. He meant the dead men. Then he looked up at Van Wert's stone face and saw no pity there. "All right. Forget the money. I can start over without it. I've done it before."

There was a pen stuck in an inkwell on the desk. Morgan watched while Van Wert got writing paper from the desk and shoved it in front of Fallon. Van Wert put the pen in his hand. Fallon looked up at him again.

"You get everything I own," Fallon said. "Land, money, stock—"

"Start writing a full confession," Van Wert said. "You know how to do it. Do it right or you'll have to do it again. Start writing. Acting in conspiracy with William Butterfield and Dave Fanshaw, I did so and so. The object of this conspiracy was, et cetera. My employee David Fanshaw hired the men who robbed the stages, so on. Also acting on my orders, Dave Fanshaw later killed three members of the gang to shut them up for good."

Van Wert looked at Morgan. "Does that cover you?"

Morgan nodded. "Better get the bodyguard in."

Van Wert prodded Fallon. "Dave Fanshaw quarreled with my bodyguard, Jimmy—write his full name—and killed him too. Fanshaw wounded me before I shot him. That should do it. Get started."

Fallon threw down the pen. "You can't expect me to confess to all that. I never ordered any killings, before or after. I never killed anybody in my life. I won't do it."

Van Wert stuck the pen back in his hand. "Write it or I'll kill you. Not just a threat. Do it right and you can run."

Fallon began to write, and as one line followed another, Morgan thought, this is like a fever dream. The room still stank of gunsmoke, the dead men lay in their blood, and the only sound was the pen scratching across the paper.

Fallon hesitated before signing his name.

Van Wert drew Fallon's gun and put it to the side of his head. "Sign it," he said.

Fallon signed the confession, and Van Wert squeezed the trigger. The bullet blew out the other side of Fallon's head. Van Wert knocked him back in the chair before blood got on the paper.

Morgan's gun was out, but Van Wert didn't look at him. He dropped Fallon's gun on the floor beside the chair. "Suicide," he said, turning toward Morgan. Put the gun away unless you plan to use it."

Morgan holstered his gun, but continued to watch Van Wert. No way to know what he'd do next. After what he'd done, who could even guess? Van Wert went to the window and looked out. "What did you do to those men out there?"

"They're tied and gagged," Morgan said. "Out cold."

"I thought you'd killed them," Van Wert said, going back to look at Fallon's body.

All Morgan felt was dull anger. "I'm no killer. What about you?"

Van Wert decided everything looked all right. "You mean Fallon?" he said. He went to Fanshaw's body and opened the bloodstained coat with two fingers. "No gun. I'll have to fix that—other things—after you leave." Next he went to where the dead gunman was sprawled behind the chair. He left things as they were.

"Killing Fallon was for the public good," he said, turning back to Morgan. "He was too slippery to let him come to trial. He bribed jurors before, he could do it again. Enough money you can do anything. I couldn't let that happen. You told Butterfield much the same thing."

Morgan knew he had. "That wasn't the same."

"How was it not? Everybody's a killer if they think it has to be done."

Morgan was angry enough to say, "Maybe you killed Fallon to cover for yourself." The minute he said it he wanted to take it back. They were all dead except Butterfield. He didn't know how he felt about Butterfield. Not right that minute.

Van Wert said, "Stop getting ready to shoot it out with me. You think I changed my mind at the last minute, is that it? Was in up to my neck, but still too much of a lawman to let them kill you?" Van Wert spat on the carpet and rubbed it with his booot. "Risk getting killed to save you, you interfering hayseed. I was ready to arrest them when you came through that goddamn window. I could have broken down Fanshaw, forced him to testify. I could have hanged Fallon."

"All right," Morgan said. "Let it go."

"Bullshit let it go. Believe me or don't, I don't give a shit." Van Wert's anger showed in his face. How real it was Morgan couldn't tell. "This thing here—Fallon. I got to know him in Illinois after he was chased out of New York. I was suspected of taking money from a bank robber I killed, that's how I got to know Fallon. They couldn't prove it, but I was shunted off to the border to chase bandits in the wilds—"

Fallon's cat jumped in the window and ran over to the body. It wandered around mewing.

Van Wert didn't want to stop talking. "Fallon knew where I was and decided I was the man to replace Jackson, who was digging too deeply into the case. Fallon knew how to pull strings, and Jackson was sent to Florida. I met Fallon in Denver before I came here. Deal was big money for me if I let the case drag. Fallon said it would be over soon, and not finding the robbers wouldn't make me look too bad. I agreed. I figured I could get all the proof I needed to put them all in jail. Then that last robbery happened just before I got here, and you got into it."

"What did you expect me to do?" Morgan was going over Van Wert's story in his mind. There were holes in it, but he wasn't about to point them out. The hell with it.

"I expected you to do what I said. But it's over now, no great thanks to you. Fanshaw—" Van Wert spat. "He brought the whole thing to a head, got himself killed. Fallon and Fanshaw, men like that, it makes you sick!"

"You think the confession will hold up." Morgan was thinking of himself. All he wanted now was to get clear of this. He still hadn't decided if he believed Van Wert, but blaming him for Margaret Deakin was stretching it.

"It'll hold up." Van Wert seemed very sure of that. "His confession, written in his own hand, signed by him, no sign of coercion, is a dying declaration, you might say. Overcome by remorse—his little friend dead—he confessed his sins and shot himself. With his record back in Albany, which I will bring up at the inquest, who will want to believe otherwise? The case will be closed except for Butterfield."

"What happens to him? He started this whole business. How do you know he's not running right now."

"He's not running anywhere. I've had a man watching him since the first day I got here." Van Wert's eyes dared Morgan to say otherwise. "Unless I have my man dead wrong, he'll make a full confession hoping to cheat the hangman. He'll blame Fallon for everything, which is right enough. Fallon was a wicked man."

Not since long-ago churchgoing days had Morgan heard anybody called wicked. Yet Van Wert spoke the word with a straight face. Either he was a hypocrite, a fanatic, or a very wicked man himself.

"What if he doesn't confess?" Morgan thought of all the old stories about the famous Jake Van Wert. Men killed in his custody, men shot down "trying to escape." Now he knew that at least some of it was true. He knew Van Wert would go after Butterfield, but what happened to him was no sure thing. Butterfield had money. . . .

The lines in Van Wert's face deepened. "He'll confess. But whatever he does he'll be made to pay. You should be made to pay—you have no respect for the law—but I'm letting you go. You have a thousand dollars that doesn't belong to you, but I'm letting you keep it."

Morgan thought of all the money Fallon said he had in his desk. Maybe it was there, probably was. Van Wert could do what he liked with it, steal it or turn it in, none of his business. But he meant to keep the thousand.

"The hell you're letting me go," he said. "I'm going anyway."

"You mean don't try to stop you?" Van Wert seemed to be considering the idea. "You mean I couldn't do it?"

"That's what I mean." Morgan got ready to draw, and maybe it was going to end here after all.

"Go back to Idaho," Van Wert said at last, keeping his hand away from his gun. "Butterfield will be dealt with, believe that if you like. But I don't want you at his trial or anywhere near it. Tend to your horses, be a sensible man, let the law take its course."

Morgan was ready to go, but he had to say one more thing. "You can believe this. If I hear Butterfield has been let down easy I'll be back."

Van Wert stared at him. "Then you'll have to face me. This time it won't be just threats. Goodbye, Morgan."

"Likewise," Morgan said, and turned his back to show Van Wert he wasn't afraid of him. It was a dumb thing to do, but he did it. He had to.

Then he climbed out the window and walked away.